Nicholas by Graham Crisp

Chapter 1. Nicholas and Ticks and Crosses

Was Nicholas Davison weird?

He didn't think he was; the only weirdness he ever experienced was in the weird boys and weird girls he had the misfortune to be at school with.

Anyway, he had Robin. He never went anywhere without Robin. Nicholas liked sitting underneath trees. There was something solid and reassuring about the thick trunk of a sturdy oak tree or the slim gracefulness of an elm. He rarely needed Robin when he was beneath a tree. He would sit for hours at a time, sometimes just gazing up at the twinkling leaves as the sunlight poked its way through the branches. Although his memory of his early childhood was somewhat hazy, this display reminded Nicholas of those cardboard tube kaleidoscopes he was sure that he played with when he was younger. Colours and shapes always fascinated Nicholas and trees and sunshine helped to satisfy his thirst. Sitting beneath trees was also a great place for Nicholas to read books. He could feel the spirit of the tree looking over his shoulders devouring the words just as a hungry dog would bolt its food. As well as being good readers, trees were also good listeners. Nicholas could sense that they liked his stories; he watched them appreciatively waving their great slender branches, rhythmically, as he narrated a particular favourite passage.

Nicholas didn't like sitting in fields. Fields were too open and exposed. Nicholas saw that cows liked fields and Nicholas didn't like cows.

Being alone and underneath a tree rendered Robin temporarily redundant and that was good. Trees plus sunlight plus books minus Robin equals good.

Was that weird? Nicholas thought not.

It was in the school playground that Robin was needed most often and nearly always when no teachers or supervisors were in the vicinity.

Nicholas hated the playground. Boys pushed and shouted stupid words to each other. It was like some strange tribal game that nearly always ended up with one of them reduced to tears and the remainder of the group laughing and pointing. Nicholas didn't like pushing and neither did he like being pushed. He knew when it was his turn to be pushed, because when the boys had got fed up with pushing each other, they turned towards him, walking slowly with narrowing eyes and maniacal stares. He would then summon Robin as their grubby hands began to unfurl, ready to begin the ritual of pushing Nicholas.

That's when Robin was at his best.

Nicholas didn't much like girls either. He would watch them huddle conspiratorially in small groups usually in the corner of the playground. They would talk furtively in whispers through cupped hands. If one of the girls spied Nicholas, and it usually was the insufferable Tracey Albourne, she would inevitably break away from the group and aim some coarse words at him and point a finger in his direction whilst glaring at him with spiteful, piercing eyes. But Nicholas never heard her words.

Robin saw to that.

At the first sign of movement from within the girls' ensemble, Nicholas positioned Robin firmly into place.

-0-

Nicholas liked the classroom. It was almost the complete opposite of the playground. No pushing, no pugnacious words and the classroom gave Nicholas something he desperately craved... Praise.

When a smiling teacher dropped his completed maths, English or science test or project onto his desk with an inevitable 'A' circled at the top in red ink, Nicholas felt warm. Sometimes the teacher would gently touch his shoulder and whisper a "well done" or something similar and soothing warmth would assemble in his stomach and flow directly upwards through his body to radiate out of his face. Nicholas was hungry for ticks and deplored crosses. Ticks were warm, crosses felt cold. Nicholas liked being warm.

Nicholas knew his classmates hated his devotion to gathering ticks. He regularly could feel a breeze of resentment blow through the room that funnelled its attention onto the back of his neck. Often Nicholas saw a flick of snake-like eyes aimed at him from Tracey Albourne whose desk was on Nicholas's left. Nicholas would glance momentarily across at the owner of the venomous eyes and catch a glimpse of her test page. A 'C+' would be circled in red ink at the top. The page would also be full of crosses; that made him shudder, crosses were evil. Nicholas would quickly turn back and look down at his ticks; that invariably brought an involuntary small smile to his lips. Behind him he could sense that the malevolent aura was growing, as more demonic crosses were handed out to the silent children behind him.

Robin was always with him in the classroom but usually held in reserve. Nicholas did keep Robin handy should the teacher leave the room. But this was a rarity; the classroom was Nicholas's domain.

Nicholas liked school work but thought that PE was pointless. He couldn't understand why anyone would want to... run... kick a ball... climb over things... jump up and down on a springy surface... or throw things to each other, or worse still, into the ground. The whirlwind of activity during a PE 'lesson' made Nicholas nauseous; cruddy smells, shouts, screams, puffy red faces, and horrible bare legs always reminded him of the time when he was taken (firmly against his will) to a football match. He endured ninety minutes of purgatory, during which he actually and shamelessly wished he was dead.

To remain sane, Nicholas pretended and reluctantly joined in this purposeless activity, pulling Robin close to him, saying to himself, *it'll be over soon, the refuge of the classroom awaits me, away from all this silliness.*

Besides, you never got a tick for doing well in PE; you just got sweaty skin and empty lungs.

Afterwards, Nicholas always took Robin into the showers with him.

-0-

Then Mr. Braithwaite arrived.

Nicholas eyed Mr. Braithwaite suspiciously. Although Mr. Braithwaite was wearing a neat, blue jacket, and taut tan trousers sporting an unbelievably sharp knife-like crease down each leg, Nicholas sensed that Mr. Braithwaite liked doing sports. His lightly bronzed skin and clear wrinkle-free complexion were the obvious danger signs. To compound Nicholas's mistrust, he spotted a thin white racket handle poking out of Mr. Braithwaite's bag that was slung against his left shoulder. To make matters worse and to Nicholas's horror, the handle was worn and well used.

Nicholas sniffed the air as Mr. Braithwaite breezed past him. It was no surprise to Nicholas that the foreboding stench of physical activity entered his widened nostrils. Nicholas felt momentarily despondent; he hunched down in the now empty corridor and rifled industriously through his bag. He pulled out his maths book and opened it. Page five was lined with ticks. Nicholas gently rubbed the page on his left cheek. That felt good; very good. Feeling more enlightened, Nicholas sighed and pushed the book back into his cavernous canvas bag. Pulling Robin close, Nicholas headed down the corridor and into the open air. It had just stopped raining. Nicholas sniffed again. "Now that's a good smell," Nicholas whispered.

-0-

Nicholas prepared two lists. Nicholas liked lists. In no particular order, Nicholas's latest list went a bit like this:

Nicholas Likes	Nicholas Dislikes
Robin	Robin
Lists	Randomisation
Trees	Fields (and cows)
Books	Television
Reading	Anything that include running & jumping etc.
Ticks (warm)	Crosses (cold)
Circled 'A's in red ink	Circled 'C+'s in red ink

Quietness	Boys
More quietness	Girls
Nice smells	Horrible smells

Nicholas was about to add some more, when he heard Mr. Braithwaite calling the class to attention. Nicholas sighed. He just knew that Mr. Braithwaite's announcement was going to be about number five on his list (running/kicking/jumping etc.).

But Nicholas was wrong.

Mr. Braithwaite was telling the class to bring in swimming gear; swim shorts, towels, goggles and ear plugs or nose clips or anything else they needed, because tomorrow Mr. Braithwaite was taking the boys swimming. (Just for balance, Miss Styles was taking the girls, Nicholas was relieved at this; Nicholas liked balance. He made a mental note to make 'Balance' number thirteen on his list. That was until he remembered that thirteen was unlucky, so he resolved to make 'Balance' 12a on his list.)

Phase One in Nicholas's life (he was in Phase Two currently) remained the favoured phase of his two phases. Although Phase One remained a bit of a blur, he knew that, in Phase One, he went swimming regularly. Nicholas liked swimming. *This should be number fourteen*, thought Nicholas. OK, so there was a bit too much bare flesh around for his liking, but as soon as Nicholas was in the pool, it was just him against the water. In deep water Nicholas's senses sharpened to the pings and plops that you never heard above the surface.

-0-

Mr. Braithwaite was asking Nicholas if he was a good swimmer. Nicholas didn't know. Nobody had ever told him. He vaguely remembered in Phase One being told that he was a 'natural', but Nicholas wasn't sure what was meant by that and he didn't ask. Much to his disappointment he hadn't been swimming in Phase Two.

Nicholas looked up at Mr. Braithwaite. He was wearing a white T shirt and blue shorts. Around his neck was a black strap holding a silver round watch with buttons on the top. Mr. Braithwaite saw Nicholas staring at the watch. He informed Nicholas that this was a stopwatch and he was going to time each boy and the one with the best time would be representing the school in September's 'Inter-School Swimming Gala'.

"Two lengths of the pool, Nicholas, there and back," explained Mr. Braithwaite.

Nicholas nodded, thinking, *Der, I know what two lengths of the pool is*. Nicholas adjusted his goggles and pulled Robin close. They would do this together.

Nicholas was restless to start. He was relieved to hear the sharp blast of Mr. Braithwaite's whistle; Nicholas dived in and swam hard.

Nicholas touched the wall of the pool and pushed his goggles up onto his forehead. A strange noise reverberated over his head. Bewildered, Nicholas hauled himself out of the pool. The strange noise continued unabated.

Cheering!
Whooping!
Clapping!

Nicholas spotted Mr. Braithwaite standing underneath the diving board surrounded by all the boys from Nicholas's class. Mr. Braithwaite was staring straight at Nicholas. He was grinning broadly and gently clapping his large hands together. All the boys were hollering and waving their hands in the air in his direction. Nicholas looked over his left shoulder. Then his right shoulder. There was no one behind him.

Nicholas turned back to face this frenzied mob. He stood still as the noisy throng, led by Mr. Braithwaite approached Nicholas. He grabbed Robin.

Mr. Braithwaite was smiling. He hushed the excited boys in his wake. Nicholas looked warily at him. With Robin at his side, he heard Mr. Braithwaite saying something along the lines of 'school record', 'fastest time he had ever recorded for a boy of Nicholas's age', 'future champion' and some other incomprehensible stuff.

Nicholas suddenly felt warm; very warm. This was just like getting a thousand ticks.

Nicholas liked being in deep water; he immediately added it to his list. It entered straight in at number one.

Chapter 2. Nicholas the 'Celeb'

Nicholas was sitting under his favourite oak tree.

Nicholas liked sitting below trees and in particular he liked sitting under this tree. When he was underneath this tree, Robin disappeared. Nicholas liked Robin, but he also liked it when Robin wasn't around.

Nicholas liked peace and quiet. Nicholas abhorred noise.
It had been raining and the thick intertwined foliage and broad gnarled branches had kept Nicholas dry. Deep in thought, Nicholas was resting his head against the trunk, his eyes half closed in rich contemplation. There was a book lying at his side with its cover facing upwards. It was titled 'Swimming in Action' by Duncan Goodhew. Nicholas wasn't enjoying this book. It featured on the front the hairless head of the author bobbing out of the water as he swam. Nicholas didn't like hairless heads. He thought they looked weird.

Mr. Braithwaite, Nicholas's teacher and swimming instructor had given Nicholas the book after their last training session. Mr. Braithwaite told Nicholas that having no hair had helped Duncan Goodhew to become a champion swimmer. Luckily, Mr. Braithwaite swiftly spotted the alarm in Nicholas's face and immediately reassured the anxious Nicholas that he wasn't suggesting that

Nicholas should shave his head.

Nicholas was relieved. He liked his hair exactly the way it was now. Nicholas liked being relieved. Nicholas didn't like being uneasy.

The past two weeks had been a bit bewildering for Nicholas. Fifteen days ago, he would be pushed and pulled in the playground by the boys and teased with spiteful words by the girls. He had to summon Robin on each occasion. Robin always did his duty, but Nicholas preferred to be left alone.

Then Mr. Braithwaite took all the boys in his class to the swimming pool and timed each boy tackling two lengths, there and back, with his shiny, silver round stop watch.

Mr. Braithwaite said Nicholas had achieved the fastest time 'by far'. Nicholas was a bit bemused by this, as all he had done was to swim as fast as he could. Nicholas's grandmother had told him to always do his best. From maths to English and now to swimming, Nicholas had obeyed her command.

Nicholas liked his grandmother and Nicholas liked obeying her orders.

Nicholas's bewilderment went a stage further when Tracey Albourne, one of a gang of girls that regularly directed a barrage of spite at Nicholas, confronted him in the school playground the day immediately after his swimming exploits.

As Tracey Albourne marched towards Nicholas, he sensed that something unfavourable was about to happen, so he immediately seized Robin. But Tracey Albourne was smiling. She called him a 'School Celeb'. Nicholas didn't know what a 'Celeb' was and he thought that is sounded like some sort of vegetable. Nicholas liked vegetables, but he didn't want to be one. However, by the look on Tracey Albourne's face a 'Celeb' must be something good. Nicholas eyed Tracey Albourne thoughtfully. He saw that she had holes pierced into her ear lobes. Nicholas could see that the piercing in each ear wasn't level. There was a lack of symmetry. Nicholas liked symmetry, Tracey Albourne's ears made him uncomfortable.

Tracey Albourne asked him, now that he was a 'Celeb', if he was going on 'Love Island'. Nicholas didn't know what 'Love Island' was. He was always confused about love. He heard a lot about love when he went to church with his grandmother, but it didn't make much sense to him. If God loved everyone, why did people die from starvation? If that was love, he preferred to stay unloved with regular meals.

But he knew that Britain was an island, so maybe that was what Tracey Albourne was referring to. Nicholas was pleased when

Tracey Albourne went back to her friends.

Nicholas didn't like Tracey Albourne, but at least he hadn't needed Robin.

Hearing a call from his grandmother, Nicholas opened his eyes and picked himself up; he grabbed his book and whistled for Robin. He headed inside. It was tea-time.

Nicholas liked tea-time.
                                    -0-
Nicholas was in Phase Two of his life. Phase One remained mostly elusive to him. He knew that he went swimming every Wednesday and once to a football match (which he hated). But in Phase Two he hadn't been swimming at all. That was until Mr. Braithwaite told him and all the other boys to bring to school their swimming gear. It was then that he became a 'School Celeb'.

In Phase Two Nicholas lived with his grandmother and grandfather. His grandmother was always busy. During the day she did 'kitchen things'. She liked baking, cooking etc. In the evenings she watched television. Nicholas didn't like television. But Nicholas did like her baking.

Nicholas's grandfather spent all day in a large leather armchair that had been placed near the French windows. His body and in particular his hands continually shook. Two women in blue tunics came into the house twice each day and took his grandfather to the bathroom. That was the only time his grandfather got out of his chair. Nicholas once asked one of the women what they were doing with his grandfather. Her reply confused Nicholas. "Sorting him out," she had said. "He has Parkinson's," she had added. Nicholas didn't know what Parkinson's was and he wondered if his grandfather could give it back to Mr. Parkinson and then stop shaking. Nicholas hoped that he wouldn't meet Mr. Parkinson because he didn't want to shake like his grandfather.

Anyway, thought Nicholas, *Robin would stop Mr. Parkinson getting near me.* Robin was good at stopping people that Nicholas didn't want to meet.

When Nicholas was in his grandmother's and grandfather's house Robin did his own thing. He wasn't needed in this cosy, warm home. But Nicholas knew he could summon Robin at any time, so if Mr. Parkinson did come knocking Robin would be there in a flash. When Nicholas came home from school, he would sit next to his grandfather as they both waited for his grandmother to bring tea and buns. His grandfather told him stories about 'The War'. He talked about the 'Gnatzees' and all the terrible things they did to Jewish people and how they dropped bombs on people's homes. Nicholas didn't know what Gnatzees were, so he typed 'What Are Gnatzees' in Google. That confused him even more. Google produced a page about different computer games and a section about a Dr. Steve Gnatz who was an orthopaedic/rehabilitation surgeon. Nicholas didn't know what an orthopaedic/rehabilitation surgeon was, but as Dr. Gnatz was pictured wearing a white coat, Nicholas assumed that he was some sort of doctor. Nicholas gazed at the picture of Dr. Steve Gnatz. He didn't look like the sort of person that would do terrible things like torturing or dropping bombs on people. Nicholas mused that perhaps Mr. Parkinson was now in Grandad's brain and was making it shake, just like his hands.

His grandfather liked a man called Winston Churchill. He said that Mr. Churchill was a hero and that he had won 'The War'. Nicholas Googled images of Winston Churchill. He was surprised to see a rather large man with a jowly face smoking a big cigar. Nicholas had expected to see a man similar to Aquaman. Nicholas liked the film Aquaman. His cousin Nancy had taken him to see the film at the cinema. Aquaman was also a hero like Mr. Churchill, but they looked very different. Nicholas didn't much like his cousin Nancy and Nicholas definitely didn't like smoking. But if Grandad said Mr. Churchill was a hero, then Nicholas was prepared to give him the benefit of the doubt.

-0-

Nicholas's grandparents didn't have a car, so Nicholas walked to school as it was just around the corner. Mr. Braithwaite picked Nicholas up each Monday to take him to the swimming pool. Nicholas had grown to like Mr. Braithwaite. Unlike a lot of adults that had been in Nicholas's life (in both Phase One and Phase Two) Mr. Braithwaite was reliable and punctual. If he said he would collect Nicholas at 4.30pm on Monday, he would arrive precisely as stated.

Nicholas liked reliability and punctuality.

Mr. Braithwaite's car had just two seats so Robin had to squeeze in between them. Nicholas didn't think that Robin liked doing this, but Robin never complained. When it was warm, Mr. Braithwaite would flick a switch on the car panel and the roof would descend. Nicholas liked roofless cars. The rush of the wind blowing his hair made him feel like his was flying. Nicholas liked the idea of flying, but he knew that humans can't fly unless they got into an aeroplane or helicopter.

-0-

Nicholas was alarmed.

Robin was next to him.

Mr. Braithwaite was in the pool with Nicholas explaining that he was going to teach him 'Breaststroke'. Now, Nicholas knew very little about ladies' anatomy, but he did know that only women have breasts. He also recalled that Tracey Albourne once said that when she was older that she was going to have a 'Boob Job'. He had heard her explain to her group of friends that a 'Boob Job' was a breast enlargement operation which would make her look 'Sexy'. Nicholas didn't want breasts or a 'Boob Job' or to look 'Sexy'. Nicholas was puzzled by Mr. Braithwaite's reaction when he told him he didn't want to learn 'Breast Stroke' as he didn't want to have breasts. Mr. Braithwaite had tears in his eyes, but not because he was sad, he seemed happy, as he was laughing, laughing and laughing.

When Mr. Braithwaite stopped laughing (which, much to Nicholas's consternation, took some considerable time), he explained to Nicholas that it was just a type of swimming stroke and no surgery or body alterations were needed.

Nicholas was comforted.

Robin sloped away.

After the swimming session was over Mr. Braithwaite drove Nicholas home. Nicholas noticed that Mr. Braithwaite would spontaneously break into a suppressed laugh. He told Nicholas that he was a 'Character'. Nicholas wasn't sure what a 'Character' was, but he quite liked the thought of being a 'Character'. Nicholas smiled. In Phase One Nicholas recalled that he smiled quite a lot. This smile may have been his first in Phase Two.

-0-

On Friday Nicholas came home from school at the usual time. His grandfather's chair was empty and there were no ladies in blue tunics in the house.

His grandmother gently touched his arm. Nicholas saw that she had red eyes. She had been crying. Nicholas immediately felt sad. She had the same expression on her face that his cousin Nancy had when Phase One ended. She explained that Grandad had gone into a hospice and was very unwell. Nicholas didn't know what a hospice was, but he sensed that it wasn't a nice place.
Nicholas didn't see his grandfather again. He sang songs in a church and people around him wore black. He was told to say his goodbyes. He clutched onto Robin as the curtains closed around a big wooden box.

He sensed that Phase Two was coming to an end and that Phase Three was about to begin.

Still, he had the 'Inter-Schools Swimming Gala' to look forward to. Mr. Braithwaite said he had 'high hopes' for him.

Nicholas didn't know what 'high hopes' were. He looked high into the tree tops but couldn't spot any hopes.

Chapter 3. Nicholas in Unusual Times
Unusual times call for unusual actions.

Normally Nicholas could only cope with one train of thought at any given time. Nicholas struggled to instruct his brain to multi-task.

But these were unusual times.

Nicholas didn't like unusual times.

Although he was still in Phase Two of his life, Nicholas sensed that Phase Three was on the horizon. This was compounded by the three things that were causing him some consternation. To simplify things Nicholas had decided to mentally list them in order of importance.

This is because Nicholas liked making lists.
1. His grandmother and her new found strange behaviour.
2. The curious regular visits to his grandmother's house by his cousin Nancy.
3. The forthcoming 'Inter-School Swimming Gala' in which Mr. Braithwaite, his teacher and swimming instructor, has 'high hopes' for him.

Nicholas settled down under his favourite oak tree. He pulled Robin close. It was unusual to need Robin when he was under this particular tree, but as he kept reminding himself, these were unusual times.

He decided to consider points one and two on his list simultaneously. Recently they had started to merge together somewhat.

Nicholas had been told that his grandfather had 'passed away'. Nicholas thought that the phrase 'passed away' was a weird choice of words. To Nicholas, the phrase seemed to imply that his grandfather was living just over the hill at the top of the road, or on the other side of the lake in Preston Park.

It was Mr. Braithwaite who explained to Nicholas that the fact was that his grandfather had died, and he would never see or speak to him again.

Nicholas liked to know 'the facts'. Mr. Braithwaite had given him 'the facts'.

That put Nicholas's mind at rest, which meant his mind was now in unison with his grandfather, as according to the card sent to his grandmother from his cousin Nancy, Grandfather was now also 'at rest'. Nicholas was relieved. He had been worried that his grandfather might be living underneath a tree on the far side of Preston Park or in a shop doorway in the High Street. Nicholas had seen figures huddled into grubby sleeping bags in the park and in the High Street shop doorways and he hated the thought that one of these people could have been his grandfather.

But since his grandfather had 'passed away', Nicholas observed that his grandmother began to act differently, and his cousin Nancy had started to visit frequently.

For reasons of efficiency Nicholas decided to use the acronyms BGD (Before Grandfather Died) and AGD (After Grandfather Died).

These were his observations:

In BGD his grandmother made cakes and baked buns.

In AGD she watched television a lot. He knew this because when he got home from school his grandmother was firmly planted on the sofa and the breakfast dishes hadn't been washed up. Also, there was no currant buns freshly baked or a sponge cake on the cake stand.

In BGD his grandmother woke early and called Nicholas for his breakfast.

In AGD she did neither. Nicholas had worked out how to set up an alarm clock he found amongst his grandfather's old things. So, at least now he could wake up, get his breakfast and then get ready for school without waking his still sleeping grandmother.

[After one of his swimming training sessions he mentioned his grandmother's BGD/AGD behaviour to Mr. Braithwaite. Nicholas saw that Mr. Braithwaite smiled when he explained what BGD and AGD meant. Mr. Braithwaite paused then replied that his grandmother was probably 'Just Grieving' and that she would soon return to normal. Nicholas didn't understand what 'Just Grieving' was, so when he got back to his grandmother's house he Googled it. But in his state of confusion Nicholas mistakenly Googled 'Just Giving' and got even more confused because he couldn't understand why his grandmother would want to run a sponsored marathon nor do a charity bike ride. He wondered what these activities had to do with a dead grandfather.]

So, Nicholas just hoped that Mr. Braithwaite was right and soon his grandmother would get back to baking buns and making cakes and preparing his breakfast.

In BGD Nicholas's grandmother did the food shopping.

In AGD they ran out of food.

Nicholas mentioned this to his cousin Nancy during her, now daily, visits to his grandmother's house. Nicholas wasn't too keen on his cousin Nancy. She was a large lady with dark curly hair and a permanent frown. She made Nicholas feel uneasy as she always seemed to be looking at him in a strange way. It was as if she was going to say something to him and then thought better of it. During her visits to his grandmother's house, he often caught her staring right at him with a slightly sad expression on her face, usually accompanied by a little shake of her head. When his cousin Nancy needed to speak to him, she loomed large over him and spoke in an exaggerated loud voice. Much to his bewilderment she always used short sentences and brusque simple words. It was if she was addressing a young child. Nicholas didn't like the way she spoke to him.

Nicholas thought that he had good reason not to be too keen on his cousin Nancy. Nicholas could sense that Robin wasn't keen on his cousin Nancy either.

But this time his cousin Nancy came good. When he told her they had no food in the house apart from three pieces of stiff bread each covered with green spots, a milk bottle that had fur inside and a tin of cat food (they didn't have a cat), his cousin Nancy acted. She asked him if he could *"USE... A... COMPUTER?"* Nicholas thought that this was a strange question. Couldn't every person of his age *'USE... A... COMPUTER?'* But he just nodded. His cousin Nancy switched on the PC they kept in the corner of the living room. She brought up a website that Nicholas saw was called Tesco. He recognised the blue and red logo from the High Street. His cousin Nancy entered a user name and password and said to Nicholas that he could order a week's worth of groceries, *"ON... HER... ACCOUNT,"* and have them, *"DELIVERED... HERE."*

As soon as Nicholas started tapping the keyboard, his cousin Nancy announced that she was going to the corner shop to *"GET... SOME... ESSENTIALS."*

Nicholas heard the door slam behind him, and began to think carefully.

There were seven days in a week and five school days. He made a list:
1. 7 breakfasts – so seven times cereal, sugar, milk, fruit juice
2. 5 school lunches – so five times bread, butter, ham, cheese, chocolate snack bars
3. 1 Saturday lunch – so one pizza, chips, salad
4. 7 evening meals – one each of meat pies, another pizza (Nicholas liked pizza), chops, sausages, baked beans, spaghetti hoops, pasta parcels
5. 1 Sunday lunch – one each of roast potatoes, stuffing, chicken, peas, carrots, gravy

Nicholas began ordering. His cousin Nancy had returned from her shopping trip and was leaning over him. She was asking him why he was mainly ordering, *"GLUTEN... FREE.... FOOD."* Nicholas replied that his grandmother had told him that Gluttony was a sin, so he made sure that wherever possible he now ate food that was free from Gluten. Nicholas saw his cousin Nancy smile. He hadn't seen her smile before. She then did her usual thing; she opened her mouth to say something then stopped. She put her hand on his shoulder which made Nicholas shudder and told him to carry on ordering.

-0-

Nicholas looked up through the branches of the trees. The bright sunshine sparkled through the leaves. This normally contented Nicholas, but these were unusual times and even the dancing sunlight bouncing off the tree's foliage couldn't settle him. He noticed that Robin had disappeared. Then he heard talking. One voice was the unmistakeable tones of his cousin Nancy, the other he wasn't too sure about. It was a man's voice. Both of the voices were coming from the patio at the rear of his grandmother's garden.

His ears sharpened at the mention of his name.

Nicholas crawled forward from behind the trunk of his tree. He saw his cousin Nancy sitting alongside the mystery man. As Nicholas emerged into the bright sunshine, they both stopped talking and simultaneously turned their heads towards where Nicholas crouched. They both gave him a quick wave. Nicholas saw his cousin Nancy nod to the mystery man and place a forefinger to her lips. He nodded back to his cousin Nancy. Then without saying another word to each other they both stood up and went inside. Nicholas saw that the mystery man was holding a black leather briefcase.

Nicholas crawled back under the tree and behind the trunk. He liked being out of sight. He still felt uneasy. Robin returned. He stayed under the tree until his cousin Nancy called him in for his tea. She said, *"YOU... HAVE... SCHOOL... TOMORROW."* Nicholas looked bemused because of course *"HE ... HAD... SCHOOL... TOMORROW."* It was Friday tomorrow; he always went to school on a Friday; except when it was a holiday and tomorrow wasn't a holiday. Nicholas liked being in class at school, but not in the playground and he didn't like holidays either.

That evening his cousin Nancy told Nicholas that, *"SHE... WAS... GOING TO... STAY WITH ... THEM... FOR - A- WHILE."* Nicholas wondered how long a 'while' was. It sounded like a long time. On Saturday morning, Nicholas watched with suspicion as his cousin Nancy hauled a large blue suitcase up his grandmother's stairs and into the 'third bedroom'.

She really was *"GOING TO... STAY WITH... THEM... FOR - A - WHILE".*

-0-

Saturday afternoon saw Nicholas back under his tree. Robin was around somewhere nearby. The sky was full of grey clouds and Nicholas was expecting rain. Nicholas liked rain but only when he was sheltered from it. Nicholas didn't like being wet, except when he was in the swimming pool. Nicholas liked the swimming pool and the thought of swimming drove his thoughts to point number three on his list.

Mr. Braithwaite had taken all the boys in Nicholas's class to the local swimming pool. He got them each to swim two lengths of the pool and told them to swim as fast as they could. In Phase One of Nicholas's life Nicholas could recall that he swam regularly, but in Phase Two he hadn't. His grandmother said that 'There was no-one to take him and she was too old'. But when he finished his two lengths, Mr. Braithwaite said he was the fastest boy 'by far' and that he would represent the school at the 'Inter-School Swimming Gala' in both 'Freestyle' and 'Breaststroke'.

Mr. Braithwaite had taught Nicholas breaststroke and he said (on more than one occasion) that he had 'high hopes' for Nicholas in the 'Inter-School Swimming Gala' which was due to be held this coming Wednesday. At first Nicholas was a little disappointed that it was going to be on a Wednesday as he had double maths on a Wednesday. Nicholas liked double maths. He always got lots of ticks during double maths. Nicholas not only liked ticks; he craved them. He often mused that his life would be meaningless if all the ticks in the world suddenly disappeared.

Nicholas trembled at the thought of a world with no ticks in his exercise books. He immediately summoned Robin.

After what Nicholas was told to be their final swimming session before the 'Inter-Schools Swimming Gala' Mr. Brathwaite asked Nicholas if he was feeling 'under any pressure' as the 'Inter-School Swimming Gala' approached. Nicholas knew that pressure was when you pressed hard down on something and as he couldn't feel anyone or anything pressing down on him, he said 'no' to Mr. Braithwaite. That seemed to please Mr. Braithwaite as Nicholas saw him nod his head and smile.

-0-

It was all over very quickly. Nicholas finished swimming both the breaststroke and freestyle. On each occasion when he touched the end of the pool, he looked up and saw the boys and girls at the far section of the gallery reserved for his school all cheering and waving at him.

Just after he had dried himself off, he was told to stand on the top and in the middle of a three sectioned podium. Two boys of similar age stood either side of him, but a little lower than him. A lady appeared with a large metal chain around her neck and big bright blue hat. She said some incomprehensible words to him and then put a round piece of metal fixed to a ribbon round Nicholas's neck. She then shook his hand. He could hear more cheering at the far end of the gallery. He was sure some were shouting his name. The lady then did the same to the two boys either side of him and moved on.

Nicholas felt curiously content. This was a good substitute for getting ticks in double maths.

But it didn't end well for Nicholas. When he was back changed into his school uniform and about to board the school minibus, Tracey Albourne, one of the spiteful girls that regularly taunted him in the playground, ran up to him. She was staring directly at him. Nicholas stood terrified. He looked for Robin. But Robin was nowhere to be found. Alarmed, Nicholas was frozen to the spot as Tracey Albourne threw her arms around his neck and proceeded to plant a firm and slightly wet kiss on his left cheek.

Tracey Albourne giggled and gripped his hand. She said something about him being a 'hero'.

Nicholas was in a state of shock.

Unusual times indeed.

Chapter 4. Nicholas and three weird things

Phase Three had started weirdly.

Nicholas was back underneath his favourite oak tree. It was early evening and Nicholas was shivering slightly, it was starting to get a little chilly. He snuggled down and pulled his grey hood tight over his head. He drew his knees up to his chin.

Robin was around somewhere. Nicholas sensed that Robin was sulking. Ever since Nicholas's outstanding success at the 'Inter-Schools Swimming Gala', things had changed. He hadn't needed to summon Robin nearly as much as before the 'Inter-Schools Swimming Gala' and Nicholas detected that Robin wasn't happy about the lack of action.

Nicholas put all thoughts about the brooding Robin to one side. He had much more important things to ponder. Three weird things had happened in the past few weeks.

Nicholas didn't like weird things.

But these three things were troubling Nicholas. He badly needed the wisdom and patience of his oak tree with its soothing sounds and fluttering leaves.

Nicholas liked order.

But more to the point Nicholas liked putting things in order. So, he gathered together the three weird things and mentally listed them in no particular arrangement of importance. Nicholas felt that each of these weird things had equal value.

His list was thus:

1. His cousin Nancy's sudden and weird change of attitude towards him
2. The weird thing that happened to him at his grandmother's funeral
3. The weird way that Tracey Albourne was acting

In a moment of madness Nicholas decided that point two should be tackled first, point one would go second and point three would remain third. He mused for a moment about rewriting his list, but he was concerned that this would take time and as it was already getting cold; soon his cousin Nancy would be calling him to come in and to get ready for bed.

So, point 2 was first.

The first weird thing about his grandmother's funeral was that it was held at a different venue to his grandfather's, who had also recently died.

He was driven to a different crematorium in a big black car, by a man wearing a black suit with a big black hat. When the car stopped outside the crematorium doors, Nicholas had felt a strange swirling feeling in the pit of his stomach. It felt as if something was alive inside him.

Nicholas didn't like this swirling feeling. It made him nauseous.

Nicholas didn't like feeling nauseous.

Nicholas climbed out of the big black car. The swirl suddenly and violently turned into a surge that began moving up his insides, slowly trying to take a hard grip of his chest.
Nicholas was about to call out to his cousin Nancy, when he felt her hand rest down hard on his shoulder. She guided him through the doors. Once inside, Nicholas felt the swirl subside slightly, allowing him to take stock of the situation and relax a little.

Curiously the place felt very familiar to Nicholas. The swirl had strangely dissipated and a wave of easiness swept over Nicholas.

He felt at home here.

Nicholas scanned the room. There was a big wooden cross in the centre on the far wall. Underneath the cross were two full length brown curtains and behind him rows of blue seats.
Nicholas felt a peculiar familiarity with these surroundings.
Nicholas noted that in front of the curtain and below the cross was a large wooden box with yellow flowers neatly arranged on top. His cousin Nancy had explained to Nicholas that the large wooden box was his grandmother's coffin. Nicholas didn't feel it necessary to explain back to his cousin Nancy that he already knew that, as she often went about explaining the blindingly obvious to him.
He just flicked a casual look at his cousin Nancy and nodded.
The man in the front, standing behind a wooden plinth, asked everyone to pray. Nicholas knew that to properly pray you had to close your eyes. At the command 'let us pray' Nicholas closed his eyes. He immediately felt an arm slip lightly around his shoulders.
Nicholas opened his right eye. His cousin Nancy was right next to him. Her eyes were closed and her hands were firmly clasped together. It wasn't her arm that went around his shoulders.
Nicholas's attention was drawn to the head of the room. He saw that there were now three wooden coffins lying in front of the curtains; two large coffins with one small one placed in between.
Nicholas stared at the three coffins. The swirl inside this stomach started up again, rising quickly towards his chest. Nicholas immediately closed his eyes again and then instantly reopened them. This time the three coffins, two large, one small, had been replaced by one large coffin and the invisible arm around his shoulder had disappeared entirely.

He shut his eyes again.

Open – three coffins, two large, one small [arm around his shoulders].

Shut.

Open – one large coffin [no arm around his shoulders].

Shut.

Open - three coffins, two large, one small [arm around his shoulders].

Shut.

Open – one large coffin [no arm around his shoulders].

Nicholas sensed a glare from his cousin Nancy. She had seen the eyes shut, eyes open routine and he could see that she wasn't happy. She mouthed, *"BEHAVE… HAVE SOME RESPECT,"* down at Nicholas. He thought about doing the eyes shut, eyes open routine one more time, but the look on his cousin Nancy's face told him that this would have been the wrong course of action.

At the end of the service, Nicholas silently slipped away and sat on a low wall in the autumn sunshine.

He did a panoramic scan around the big, brown brick building with its green gardens adorned with small bouquets of brightly coloured flowers. The swirl reappeared in his stomach.

Nicholas inexplicably sensed he had been here before. Was it in Phase One? Much to Nicholas's regret he could never remember much about Phase One of his life. He could remember going swimming regularly and that it had been a happy phase. However, he could just about recall that it had some sort of a sad ending, but not much beside. It was if someone had uploaded a firewall in his brain that was blocking out data about his life in Phase One.

Nicholas knew that the only way to remove the firewall was to find the user name and password and uninstall it.

He was about to try when Nicholas heard his name being called. He trudged slowly back to the big black car. As the car drove away Nicholas looked over his shoulder at the building.

He HAD been here before.

-0-

It was now getting quite cold. The oak tree continued to do its duty.

Robin was somewhere around and still brooding.

Nicholas's mind moved onto point two. After the death of his grandmother, his cousin Nancy had told him that she was going to move into Nicholas's grandmother's house. She informed Nicholas that this arrangement was, *"NOT... FOREVER... BUT UNTIL... HE... FINISHED... SCHOOL."*

Nicholas resolved this was the precise moment when Phase Three officially began. His grandmother's funeral was just the preliminary stage designed to get him acclimatised.

It was on the Wednesday after his grandmother's funeral, when Nicholas arrived back to his grandmother's house, after school, and saw that his cousin Nancy was wearing her 'going out' clothes. She announced that she had booked an appointment to see Mr. Braithwaite, Nicholas's teacher and swimming coach.

Nicholas was puzzled why his cousin Nancy wanted to meet Mr. Braithwaite, but he didn't ask why and his cousin Nancy didn't say why. She buttoned up her coat and told him, *"NOT TO ANSWER ...THE DOOR... TO... ANY STRANGERS... WHILST SHE... WAS AT HIS... SCHOOL."*

Nicholas shut the door behind her and skipped into the lounge. He settled down in his grandmother's best-loved armchair and picked up his favourite book - *Percy Jackson and the Greek Gods*. Nicholas liked reading about Greek Gods. Nicholas identified as the Greek God Poseidon – the protector of all waters.

He was deep into the adventures of Percy Jackson, when his cousin Nancy disturbed his train of thought by tapping him gently on his shoulder. Nicholas immediately saw that she looked different. Her frown had mellowed and she was smiling at him. Her touch felt light and friendly.

Nicholas liked light and friendly but he wasn't expecting that this delightful duo would ever come from his cousin Nancy.
She asked him to, "Put that book down for a moment." Nicholas immediately noticed that her voice was different. Normally she would have said, *"NICHOLAS... PUT...THAT... BOOK DOWN."* But just like her touch, her voice had become light and friendly.

She told Nicholas that he was a 'dark horse'.

Nicholas knew he wasn't anything like a dark horse. For a start he was a human and rather light coloured, with two legs and not four. He couldn't jump fences either.
His cousin Nancy carried on talking to him. She used phrases like 'you're a genius' and 'a straight A student' adding that he was 'a potential Olympic swimmer' and that he could go to a place called Oxbridge. Nicholas hadn't heard of a place called Oxbridge. Did she mean Uxbridge? Nicholas knew that was somewhere near London. He was about to tell her that he preferred to go to places that he had heard of when his cousin Nancy shushed him, saying that she was going to 'encourage him to reach his full potential', adding somewhat curiously, 'after all that had happened to him in the past' and that she was going to ensure that he 'got on'.

Nicholas wasn't sure what he was supposed to 'get on'.

Maybe she meant the dark horse.

-0-

The wind was starting to blow hard now, and the tree's leaves were fluttering angrily, as if they were annoyed by this unwelcome intrusion. Nicholas was getting colder and considered going inside. His cousin Nancy was being extra nice to him. She always made him a hot chocolate before he went to bed as 'chocolate drinks will help him get a good night's sleep'.

Nicholas liked hot chocolate and a good night's sleep.

Nicholas was starting to like his cousin Nancy.
But rather than sample the delights of his cousin Nancy's hot chocolate, Nicholas turned his final thoughts to point three on the list; the redoubtable Tracey Albourne and her recent weird behaviour.

It all started on a Tuesday when Nicholas was walking home after school. Some of the students hung around chatting after school, but

Nicholas always left promptly.
Nicholas liked punctuality.

As he walked, he felt a sharp jab into his right shoulder, and turning, he saw the smiling face of Tracey Albourne. She asked if she could walk along with him. Instinctively Nicholas looked around for Robin. But Robin was still sulking and nowhere to be found. Tracey Albourne didn't wait for Nicholas's reply to her request, but she just grabbed his arm and began talking.

Nicholas soon discovered that Tracey Albourne liked talking.

Nicholas was amazed about how much she knew about his fellow female school friends.

By the time he had got to the corner of the street where they both lived, he had learned five things about six different girl students in his year.

Nicholas quickly made one of his mental lists and added his notes alongside each discovery.

1. Mandy Johnson put grey socks in her bra. *[Grey socks were more useful on your feet than in a bra.]*
2. Louise Charlton got 'hammered' on red wine. *[A hammer is for knocking nails into wood. Red wine was given out in church communion.]*
3. Libby Acton and Nadia Kowalski had been seen kissing each other in the girls' toilets and they were probably 'Lezzies'. *[He had an Aunt Lizzie, but he hadn't seen her kissing another female.]*
4. Paula Evans had two dads but no mother because they were 'gay'. *[Two dads would be great; they could each take him swimming twice a week. Gay was a nice word.]*
5. Cindy Allsopp was an 'Annie' because she didn't eat lunch and was very thin. *[How could Cindy become an Annie when her name was Cindy? Lunch was good for you as it helped your brain function in the afternoon. So now he knew why Cindy got lots of crosses and very few ticks in afternoon Maths.]*

Tracey Albourne waved to Nicholas and headed towards her own home. Nicholas felt exhausted; his right ear was actually numb.

-0-

It was now very cold; the wind blew relentlessly.
Nicholas could hear the shrill tones of his cousin Nancy calling him inside. He had one final thought about Tracey Albourne.

He had overheard her say to Mandy Johnson (the girl with the grey socks) during morning break, that Nicholas Davison was not 'weird'. He was 'cute'.

-0-

As Nicholas brushed his teeth, he stared hard into the bathroom mirror.

Is that face 'cute'? He thought.

Was Nicholas Davison 'cute'?

Tracey Albourne thought so.
Nicholas liked being 'cute'.

Nicholas was beginning to like Tracey Albourne.

Nicholas had a good night's sleep. The hot chocolate and being 'cute' worked. Tracey Albourne's startling revelations about his fellow students had removed all thoughts about the three coffins (two large and one small, in between) he had seen in the crematorium.

But somehow, he knew that they would return.

Chapter 5. Nicholas and a grade 'D' minus

Normally at this time of the evening, Nicholas would be sitting under his favourite oak tree either carefully pondering recent events or reading one of his many books on his favoured subject, Greek Gods.

In this usual environment, Robin would be nearby and the steady fluttering of the tree's leaves gently swaying in a light breeze would help Nicholas to bring some order into his life.

Nicholas liked order.

But this evening was different.

What happen to Nicholas yesterday was very different.

Nicholas's thoughts were usually centred on schoolwork, school life, swimming and his home life with his cousin Nancy. But yesterday's event had made him add an extra dimension to his daily reflections and that had made Nicholas uncomfortable. Was Phase Four about to begin when Phase Three had barely got underway?

The phases in Nicholas's life were important to him, but maddeningly Phase One continued to stay a mystery to him. He could recall some moments, but somehow the majority of Phase One remained compacted deep down. When Nicholas was musing the phases in his life, he always made an attempt to download Phase One. Quickly, Nicholas tried in vain to bring Phase One out into the open, but as always, the firmly constructed firewall blocked him. He made a weak attempt to find the username and password, but he knew that this would need a gargantuan effort and Nicholas didn't have the time. He needed to concentrate hard on more current, pressing events.

So, Nicholas gave up on Phase One (again).
He decided to leave the comfort of the tree and take a solitary quiet walk around the lake in nearby Preston Park. He considered that it would be a soothing contrast to his usual routine and anyway Robin was no longer around. Robin had slipped away from Nicholas almost unnoticed. Nicholas's new status as a school and county swimming champion, along with Tracey Albourne's fierce defence of him at every opportunity, meant that Robin's skills were becoming increasingly redundant. Nicholas sensed that Robin was aware of this. There were no goodbyes, just an acceptance that a parting of the ways was best for both.

In many ways Nicholas was relieved that Robin had gone. Although Robin had been a champion defender and a source of great comfort to Nicholas, his life and, particularly his school life, had changed. His swimming exploits had almost single-handedly raised the profile of the school. Nicholas felt that this had resulted in more respect from his fellow students. Besides, they were all getting older and more mature. There was considerably less pushing and pulling in the playground.

Nicholas liked being relieved. Nicholas liked being respected. Stopping at the water's edge, Nicholas looked down into the bluish green water of Preston Park Lake; he could just about make out the slightly comical wavering image of his face in the clear water. He smiled to himself; his reflection exactly mirrored his current thought processes.
As he continued to gaze into the lake, his mind travelled backwards to recent events.

-0-

Tracey Albourne, previously his playground nemesis, had taken to walking home with Nicholas each day after school.

Nicholas had grown to like her cheery company. She always swung on his arm and pranced alongside him, telling him tales of gossip and scandal that normally involved female students at their school. Her bright eyes shone into his as she talked.

Nicholas liked bright eyes.

Nicholas liked Tracey Albourne's bright eyes.

Nicholas was always surprised just how much she knew about other students' lives. It struck him just how little he knew his fellow scholars. But sometimes Tracey Albourne had to admit that she got some bits wrong. Nicholas recalled the time she accused Nadia and Libby of being 'lezzies' because they had reportedly been seen kissing each other. However, Nadia was now going out with Jack Lansley, a big brute of a guy, who excelled in rugby, so reports of her inclination towards homosexuality had been redacted.
Or exaggerated, or never happened, thought Nicholas.

Their walk home was always a happy affair. It was a perfect end to a school day. Tracey Albourne positively twinkled. She was upbeat and had a super-charged outlook on life. As they parted at the end of Nicholas's Street, she always reached up and gave Nicholas a simple peck on his left cheek, squeezing his arm, repeating each time, 'see you tomorrow, same time same place'.

Nicholas liked repetition.

That was until the day before yesterday.
T
racey Albourne was waiting for Nicholas on the low stone wall that surrounded the school. The last few students were slowly drifting away from the school gates. Nicholas had been held up after lessons by Mr. Braithwaite who was briefing him about the forthcoming 'Under Seventeen County Swimming Championships'. Nicholas was competing and was expected to win in both the breaststroke and freestyle races.
Nicholas had finally broken away from Mr. Braithwaite and spied Tracey Albourne sitting on the wall. He hurried over to where she was sitting. As he approached her, Nicholas saw that instead of the bright, cheery wave she usually reserved for him, she just glanced up at him and forced a weak smile. Nicholas sensed that she was troubled. He felt awkward. Not knowing what to say, he just lifted her up gently by her elbow and they began walking quietly towards their respective homes. After a few moments Tracey Albourne broke the silence. She said she was sick of 'being thick'.

Nicholas had only vaguely considered Tracey Albourne's body. He had always preferred to look into her eyes. But he didn't think she was thick. In fact, he thought she was rather thin. Tracey Albourne sensed that she hadn't made herself clear to Nicholas. She dug her hand into her left pocket and pulled out a piece of paper and thrust it under Nicholas's nose.

Nicholas stopped and examined the paper. He recognised it immediately; it was a maths test he had completed last year. He had got an 'A' star; 100% correct answers. Tracey Albourne had got 'D' minus; 10% correct answers. Nicholas physically shivered when he saw how many crosses Tracey Albourne had got on her test paper.

Nicholas pondered how he could help her. He suddenly found himself inviting Tracey Albourne to his grandmother's house tomorrow evening for some 'extra maths tuition'. He went on to say (unnecessarily as Tracey Albourne already knew he was brilliant at maths) that maths was his favourite subject and one at which he excelled.
Tracey Albourne agreed to his suggestion without any hesitation. He was heartened when he saw that the familiar Tracey Albourne smile had returned to her lips. Nicholas glowed. They parted, as usual, on the corner of his street, but this time her customary peck on his cheek lingered a little longer and it decidedly felt more moist than usual. Being ever the diplomat, Nicholas waited until Tracey Albourne was out of sight before he wiped his cheek.

-0-

Nicholas had said to Tracey Albourne that she should be at his grandmother's house at 6.30pm. He watched the clock in the living room. It was 6.32pm and there was no sign of Tracey Albourne. Nicholas was irritated. Nicholas liked punctuality and Tracey Albourne wasn't being punctual.

At 6.35pm Nicholas heard the doorbell ring. He dashed to the door and opened it. He was just about to admonish her for being late when his eyes widened. He instinctively rubbed them. It was definitely A Tracey Albourne standing in the doorway, but it wasn't THE Tracey Albourne that walked home with him from school. This new Tracey Albourne had long brown hair loose around her shoulders. She had deep red lips, darkened eyes and a hint of pink on her cheeks. Instead of the usual bottle green school dress, this Tracey Albourne was wearing a pair of tight denim jeans held up by a large black belt, sporting an oversized silver buckle. Her blue loose cotton top bore the word 'LEGEND' across the front.

A large blue and white striped bag was slung across her shoulders. He could just spot the words 'Mathematics Homework' written across the top of a school exercise book that was poking out of the bag.

She had turned her left cheek towards Nicholas. He could hear her saying, "Well aren't you going to kiss me hello?"

Nicholas liked this new Tracey Albourne.

He really, really liked this new Tracey Albourne.

Nicholas kissed the proffered pink cheek.

He invited her inside.

As she squeezed past the bedazed Nicholas, a delightful waft of sweet perfume breezed into his nostrils rendering him momentarily light-headed. Looking over the head of Tracey Albourne and down the hallway, Nicholas spotted his cousin Nancy lurking in the kitchen doorway. He saw her give him an exaggerated wink, followed by a swift thumb's up. Nicholas's face reddened. He showed Tracey Albourne into the lounge and followed her in.

Nicholas was pleasantly surprised how attentive Tracey Albourne was as they went through her 'D' minus test paper. Nicholas patiently explained how to work through each module and how each correct answer was reached. He set her a short exercise. As she worked, he gazed across the table at her and saw a determined look on her face and intent in her eyes that he had never experienced before. She looked wise and thoughtful, almost the opposite of the 'Tigger-like', bouncy, gossipy girl that walked with him after school. This made Nicholas happy.

In all they spent an hour and a half reviewing her test paper and Tracey Albourne nodded solemnly when Nicholas asked her if she now understood the vagaries of mathematical equations and if she would now feel more confident when she had to sit her next test paper. Nicholas watched her smile and then felt her hand on his. She was thanking him calling him a 'genius' and a 'brilliant teacher'.

Nicholas felt warm.

Nicholas liked feeling warm. Tracey Albourne made him warm.

Nicholas liked the fact that Tracey Albourne made him warm.

With the maths 'lesson' now closed, Nicholas and Tracey Albourne sat slightly awkwardly side by side on the settee. His cousin Nancy had slid into the lounge carrying a tray of fairy cakes and a jug of orange juice. Much to both Nicholas and Tracey Albourne's chagrin, they spotted three glasses on the tray. His cousin Nancy poured out three tumblers of juice and sat down in Nicholas's grandmother's favourite chair. She offered the pair a fairy cake each. They accepted one each. It was agonising as they both listened to his cousin Nancy asking banal questions to Tracey Albourne on the lines of such 'where do you live?' 'How long have you lived there?' and, 'What do you plan to do when you leave school?' She prattled on for what seemed like an eternity. Nicholas was hugely impressed in the way that Tracey Albourne batted away each of his cousin Nancy's enquiries with the skills of a seasoned test opening batsman.

They both gave a huge sigh of relief when his cousin Nancy got up and took the tray into the kitchen. Nicholas and Tracey Albourne looked at each and spontaneously burst into a fit of giggles. Nicholas said that his cousin Nancy meant well, but she wasn't used to him bringing friends back here, hence the 'twenty questions'. Tracey Albourne assured Nicholas that she didn't mind and was quite flattered by his cousin Nancy's attention. She laughed and gripped his hand tightly.

The lounge clock showed 9.15pm and Tracey Albourne said she had to go home. As she rose from the settee, she spotted Nicholas's book; 'The Complete Guide to Greek Gods and Goddesses, Monsters, Heroes, and the Best Mythological Tales!'

"Yours?" she enquired. Nicholas nodded. Nicholas watched intently as Tracey Albourne flicked through the pages of his book.

As he gazed at Tracey Albourne, he said to himself, *Aphrodite*. Poseidon had found his Aphrodite.

Tracey Albourne put the book down on the arm of the settee, Nicholas heard her say something like 'you'll have to teach me more about these Gods of yours'. Nicholas said he would like to do that. But now it was time for her to go home.

Nicholas said he would walk her to the end of the street, just to make sure 'she got home safely'.

Tracey Albourne was about to say no, but she caught a look in Nicholas's eyes that cautioned her from speaking.

They walked up the street in silence, Tracey Albourne held Nicholas's arm tightly. When they reached the top, they turned to each other; Tracey Albourne was just about to open her mouth to speak, when Nicholas bent down and delicately cupped both of her cheeks in his hands. He kissed her on the lips. He had recently been forced by his cousin Nancy to watch a romantic film in which there were many kissing scenes. Nicholas thought that this would be the right moment to kiss Tracey Albourne and much to Nicholas's delight/relief she responded enthusiastically. After what seemed like a lifetime to Nicholas, their mouths separated.

Nicholas felt a strange combination of exhaustion and a sensation that he never encountered before. Tracey Albourne said she was in 'ecstasy'. Nicholas didn't think that he had ever experienced ecstasy.

But he had now.

Nicholas liked ecstasy.

After a moment's silence, they both agreed that this easily was the best maths lesson either of them had ever had.

Tonight, one plus one had definitely equalled two.

-0-

With his thoughts now back in some sort of order, an inwardly smiling Nicholas, rose from his haunches and turned his back on Preston Park Lake. Dusk was drifting down and an autumnal twang was in the air. But Nicholas was oblivious to both. He was warm inside.

Tracey Albourne had made him warm.

But Nicholas didn't like Tracey Albourne anymore.

.

.

.

.

.

He loved her.

Chapter 6. Nicholas Goes Budgie Smuggling

Nicholas was upstairs in his bedroom. He was diligently packing his swimming gear. Today was Saturday and this was to be his third Saturday training session with his new swimming coach, Mr. Fahey. Nicholas was unsure about Mr. Fahey, who introduced himself as Joe and insisted that Nicholas addressed him as Joe.

Nicholas didn't like calling adults by their first name and anyway Mr. Fahey didn't look like a Joe.

Mr. Fahey [call me Joe] was a short rotund man with a bald head and ruddy cheeks. He seemed to be always wearing the same grey tracksuit trousers and blue sweatshirt. He carried a whistle tied to a piece of string around his neck. Curiously, Nicholas had never seen Mr. Fahey [call me Joe] blow his whistle. He wondered why Mr. Fahey [call me Joe] wore it.

Mr. Fahey [call me Joe] had been recommended to Nicholas by his teacher and part-time swimming instructor, Mr. Braithwaite. He told Nicholas that Mr. Fahey [call me Joe] was a highly respected swimming coach with years of experience who could take Nicholas to the next level.

Nicholas wasn't sure where the next level was. He didn't want to go too high as he had, in the past, suffered a dizzy spell when he was made to walk across a rope bridge over a deep ravine on a school outbound day. Nicholas quite liked the level he was on now, namely ground level.

Mr. Braithwaite said that Mr. Fahey [call me Joe] would introduce new techniques to Nicholas which would make him a better swimmer. But so far, the only new technique that Mr. Fahey [call me Joe] had introduced, was his ability to shout repeatedly at Nicholas from the side lines to 'hit the water 'aard'.
Nicholas didn't like 'hitting the water 'aard'. He just swam as fast as he could.

With the words 'hit the water 'aard' now stuck in his head, Nicholas began to pack his kit.

He always packed his kit from the list indelibly printed in his mind:
1. Swimming trunks (Blue)
2. Spare swimming trunks (Black)
3. Blue and white striped towel
4. Spare red and white striped towel
5. Shower Gel at least half full
6. Ear plugs
7. Spare ear plugs
8. Swimming goggles
9. Spare swimming goggles
10. Swimming cap (white)
11. Spare swimming cap (dark blue)

He packed all eleven items into his green canvas bag in list order. The blue swimming trunks placed at the bottom and the spare dark blue swimming cap on the top.

Nicholas's ears pricked up. He could hear Tracey Albourne talking downstairs. She was either speaking on her mobile or with his cousin Nancy. Unable to determine who she was speaking to, Nicholas finished packing his kit.

Satisfied that all was in order, Nicholas zipped up his bag and slung it over his right shoulder. He then stopped and put his bag down on the bed and reopened it. He checked through all the items before zipping it back up for a second time. Now completely satisfied all was definitely in the right order, Nicholas made his way to the stairs.

Nicholas liked things in the right order.

Tracey Albourne was still speaking when he started descending the stairs.

He watched her as she danced around the hallway, her mobile telephone pressed hard against her left ear. She was wearing her trademark tight blue denim jeans and a white T shirt with the word FIERCE written across the front in blue script. Nicholas paused for a moment. He nodded and smiled when he saw that she was wearing his favourite pink Nike trainers.

Tracey Albourne and Nicholas Davison was an official 'item'.

Nicholas liked being part of an item. Nicholas really liked being part of an item with Tracey Albourne.

Their romantic alignment was sealed the moment after they kissed following Nicholas's impromptu maths lesson. Initially they kept their arrangement private. They enjoyed having a secret between themselves; it made them both feel special that they knew something that the other students at their school knew nothing about. But when they were spotted huddled together in an unmistakeable amorous embrace in Preston Park by fellow student, Mandy Johnson, the word soon spread.

The boys in his year were aghast. They couldn't fathom how a 'geeky weirdo' like Nicholas Davison had 'pulled' a 'babe' like Tracey Albourne. The girls were equally appalled how the 'Queen Bee' of their 'Posse' could get herself tangled up with a guy like Nicholas Davison. Although during their discussions on the Tracey Albourne/Nicholas Davison hook up, Libby Acton observed that ever since Nicholas had been training hard for his swimming competitions, he had 'toned up' a bit; quite a bit in fact, reflected Libby.

Tracey Albourne saw Nicholas coming down the stairs. She said her 'goodbyes' and clicked her 'phone off. "My mum," she told Nicholas. "She's going out with that loser Toby again tonight," she added, slightly shaking her head and rolling her eyes.
Nicholas nodded.

He had only met Tracey Albourne's mother once. She was another adult that insisted that he called her Sharon and not Mrs. Albourne. Nicholas didn't want to call her Sharon, but Tracey Albourne told him to go with it as it was 'easier'. Nicholas wasn't sure what was easier, but he liked to please Tracey Albourne, so Mrs. Albourne was now a 'Sharon'.

Nicholas was about to shout his own 'goodbyes' to his cousin Nancy, when he spotted her in the kitchen. She was not alone. Sitting opposite her on the far side of the kitchen table was a man that Nicholas remembered seeing before. Nicholas thought for a second. It came back to him. This was the same man that he had seen in conversation with his cousin Nancy, in the back garden, several months ago. They had both stopped talking when they spied him watching them from underneath the oak tree.

This time, the man had the same black briefcase resting against the leg of the kitchen table and a batch of typewritten A4 papers were strewn across the table. His cousin Nancy had a pen in her hand. Just as before, as soon as they saw Nicholas, they stopped talking. The man quickly gathered the papers together and hurriedly lent down and stuffed them into the black briefcase. His cousin Nancy waved him away, saying, "Off you go, Nicholas, or you'll be late for your training." The man waved at Nicholas. Nicholas waved back. He felt Tracey Albourne grab his hand. They both left the house and went off towards the High Street to catch the number 42 bus that took them to Neptune Swimming Pool.

As they sat on the front two seats of the number 42 bus, Nicholas pondered for a few moments. Who was the man with the papers and briefcase and why a second visit to his cousin Nancy? His train of thought was cursorily taken away from men and black briefcases as Tracey Albourne began telling Nicholas that Nadia Kowalski and Jack Lansley had now 'split up'. According to Louise Charlton, Nadia had told her that Jack loved rugby more than Nadia. Apparently, Nadia was 'cut-up' about the 'break-up'.

Nicholas knew that this wasn't true, because he had seen Nadia just yesterday and she was completely in one piece. There were no signs of any cuts. *But*, he thought, *how could anyone love a game more than a girl?*

Nicholas liked swimming, but he loved Tracey Albourne.

As Tracey Albourne carried on talking on about the now non-relationship between Nadia Kowalski and Jack Lansley, Nicholas's thoughts turned to the first time Tracey Albourne asked if she could go with him to one of his swimming sessions. Nicholas was puzzled at this request. He couldn't understand why she would want to stand at the side of a pool in a chlorine heavy atmosphere just to watch him going up and down.

She replied that she wanted to see him, 'close up', in his 'budgie smugglers'.

Nicholas liked birds in trees, but not in cages. Anyway, there was no need to smuggle budgerigars as you could buy them in most pet shops. Nicholas noticed that every time Tracey Albourne said 'budgie smugglers' she put her hand to her mouth and giggled. This made Nicholas curious, so he Googled 'budgie smugglers.' Nicholas had reddened when he read the descriptions of 'budgie smugglers'. He never mentioned to Tracey Albourne that he had discovered what 'budgie smugglers' were, but he couldn't help feeling a little self-conscious the first time he stepped out of the changing room in her presence.

The number 42 bus was about to pull up at their stop. He felt Tracey Albourne nudge him and say, "Well, what do you think about it?" Nicholas didn't know what 'to think about it' as he hadn't been paying any attention. They got off the bus and went up the stone steps and into the Neptune Swimming Pool. Tracey Albourne was just behind him. He heard her let out a big sigh and then he felt a friendly jab in his back.

-0-

Nicholas was pulling on his clothes in the tiny changing room. His ears were buzzing. He was musing over the session he had just completed. Mr. Fahey [call me Joe] had added another technique to his, so far, singular repertoire. During freestyle practice Mr. Fahey [call me Joe] repeatedly shouted 'hit the water 'aard!' Whereas during breaststroke he now burst into 'push 'aard' at regular intervals.

Normally, Nicholas liked consistency, but 'hitting the water 'aard' and 'push 'aard' had very little meaning to him. He just swam as fast as he could. But, Mr. Fahey's [call me Joe] techniques must be working because he informed Nicholas at the end of today's session that he had twice broken the junior school record in both the freestyle and breaststroke disciplines. As he was leaving the pool to get dried, Mr. Fahey [call me Joe] gently tapped Nicholas on his bare shoulder and muttered a concrete 'well done' and a slightly abstract 'you're getting there'. As far as Nicholas was concerned, he wasn't going anywhere.

Nicholas was tying up his laces when he heard a sharp tap on the changing room door and Tracey Albourne's distinctive voice on the other side. Nicholas liked hearing Tracey Albourne's voice. She was telling him to 'hurry up' and that she was going to buy him a 'Mackie Dee' at the restaurant across the road from the Neptune Swimming Pool. He replied that he was 'just coming'. He was sure that she had just called him 'sweetie'.

Nicholas didn't normally identify as a 'sweetie', but he liked the idea of being Tracey Albourne's 'sweetie'.

-0-

The couple sat opposite each other in a practically deserted restaurant. Tracey Albourne was alternatively nibbling on a Big Mac or sucking on a straw that was pushed through a lid and into a paper container half full with strawberry milkshake. Nicholas had already eaten his burger and was finishing off a carton of orange juice.

Nicholas was watching Tracey Albourne eat and drink. Nicholas spent quite a lot of time observing her. He noted that she had any number of individual traits. But the one attribute that stood out above all the others, was if she was about to ask him a difficult question, like, 'when was the last time you cried?' or 'which other girls have you kissed?' she always put her right hand up to her mouth and lightly scratched her top lip. (By the way, the answer to the questions was 'probably when he was a baby' and 'none'.) Tracey Albourne put her burger down and sucked up the remnants of her milkshake. She looked directly at Nicholas and put her right hand to her mouth and scratched her top lip. *Here it comes,* thought Nicholas, hoping the question that was coming wasn't anything to do with 'other girls'.

Nicholas was momentarily speechless. Tracey Albourne's difficult question wasn't anything to do with something simple like 'other girls', but a much harder question.

"How come you live with your cousin Nancy and not with your mum or dad?"

Nicholas couldn't answer her question. He didn't know the answer to her question. Nicholas felt a swirling deep in his stomach. The something was awakening. It was exactly the same feeling he had experienced during his grandmother's funeral.

Nicholas felt nauseous. He got up from the table and went outside. Tracey Albourne followed directly behind him; her half-eaten burger remained grasped tightly in her hand.

Chapter 7. Nicholas and Mrs. Baines

Nicholas was in his bedroom. He was lying face up on his bed and staring blankly at his bedroom ceiling.

Nicholas was glum.

Nicholas didn't like being glum.

Right out of the blue his girlfriend, Tracey Albourne, had been whisked away by her mother Sharon to spend a WHOLE TWO WEEKS in the south of France visiting her auntie.

This was the first time they had been apart since they became an item some six months previously. Nicholas liked being part of an item and in particular an item that involved Tracey Albourne.
To compound their agony, her mother Sharon had put severe limits on the use of Tracey Albourne's phone. She told Nicholas, "It's going to be a girls' fortnight, so no calls, and texting or WhatsApp messaging, you'll have plenty to catch up on when she gets back." She told her daughter to 'Stop Brooding'.

Nicholas thought that only hens got broody, so he wondered by her mother Sharon was likening Tracey Albourne to a hen. She looked and acted nothing like a hen. She didn't have wings or a beak and she talked and not clucked.

Actually she talked quite a lot.

Nicholas liked hearing Tracey Albourne talking. Nicholas was going to miss hearing Tracey Albourne talking.

Pulling himself up into a sitting position, Nicholas decided it was time to put his glumness to one side and concentrate on his second favourite pastime; swimming.
With a monumental effort he forcibly pushed Tracey Albourne and her 'girls' fortnight' to the back of his mind and turned the front of his mind to two matters that were swirling around his head. The first was his new swimming coach and the second concerned the weird way his cousin Nancy had reacted to this new appointment.
Mr. Fahey (who insisted that Nicholas called him Joe) his swimming coach, had successfully guided Nicholas through qualification to the national swimming championships, during which Nicholas broke the British junior records in both the freestyle (400 metres) and breaststroke (200 metres) disciplines.

Afterwards, Mr. Fahey [call me Joe] informed Nicholas that he was easily ready for the national swimming championships which were set to be held in six months' time in Glasgow. But for Nicholas to be really successful in these championships, Mr. Fahey [call me Joe] said he needed specialist coaching. He told Nicholas that the university in the next town to where Nicholas lived had an accredited swimming centre of excellence and the head of the centre, a Mrs. Maureen Baines, had already taken a keen interest in Nicholas. Mr. Fahey [call me Joe] asked Nicholas if he could pass on Nicholas's contact details so that she could get in touch. Nicholas nodded his ascent.

Nicholas was keen to have a new coach.

Nicholas had never really taken to Mr. Fahey [call me Joe]. He certainly wouldn't miss his continual shouting 'hit the water 'aard' (freestyle) and 'push 'aard' (breaststroke), which were the only methods of coaching that Mr. Fahey [call me Joe] seemed to possess. However, they parted company amicably with a handshake and mutual best wishes.

The very next day Nicholas received a text from Mrs. Baines with an invitation to him and his cousin Nancy [as she was his guardian], to meet up with her for a tour of the university's facilities. Preferring to talk rather than just return a text, he immediately called Mrs. Baines and set up the appointment.

When Nicholas arrived back from school, he found his cousin Nancy in the kitchen preparing their tea. He told her the news. Nicholas expected his cousin Nancy to be pleased, but when he told her about the invitation to visit the university and the meeting with Mrs. Baines, he saw that she became decidedly uncomfortable. She replied, "Newham University?" When Nicholas affirmed, he saw her face visibly droop. Oddly, she began fidgeting with her necklace and twisting her fingers through the folds of her skirt. Nicholas studied her face. Her expression was more anxious than angry and much to Nicholas's astonishment, she suddenly blurted out 'was he sure that he wanted to do this?' and 'perhaps he should consider concentrating more on his academic studies'.

Nicholas was momentarily speechless. He felt a sudden upsurge of emotion that almost made him tearful. Nicholas composed himself. He couldn't look his cousin Nancy directly in the eye, but Nicholas stood his ground. He told her quite forcibly that he was going to meet Mrs. Baines and she could come with him or not, that was her choice.

This confrontation left Nicholas exhausted. He ran up to his bedroom. He had never spoken to his cousin Nancy in that manner and it disturbed him. In fact, he couldn't recall ever speaking to anyone so forcibly. He grabbed his mobile telephone and sent a text to Tracey Albourne telling her of his confrontation with his cousin Nancy. She replied immediately with an 'astonished face' and a 'thumbs up' emoji.

Her curt response bothered Nicholas.

Nicholas didn't like curt responses.

Then he remembered that Tracey Albourne's mother Sharon had imposed a draconian limit on her phone usage whilst she was away visiting her aunt in France.

Nicholas removed 'bothered' from his thoughts.

From inside his bedroom, Nicholas heard the front door close. He rose and looked out of his bedroom window. He just managed to catch a glimpse of his cousin Nancy's car heading away up the street. He ran downstairs and saw a note pinned to the inside of the front door.

'I've gone to visit cousin Billy. I will be staying there for a few nights. I'll probably be back on Tuesday. There's plenty of food in the fridge. See you soon Nancy xx'.

Nicholas rubbed his nose.

The last time he had met his cousin Billy was at his grandmother's funeral. Cousin Billy was a slender man, probably aged in his late forties, with thin grey hair. Nicholas recalled that his cousin Billy's face remained in a permanent scowl all through the service and afterwards. Aside from his cousin Nancy, he spoke very little to any of the other mourners. Nicholas remembered seeing the two of them in a close, whispered, conversation in the garden after most of the other people had left. They both bore serious expressions. Nicholas had no idea why his cousin Nancy should want to stay with his cousin Billy, but he sensed that this clearly had something to do with his proposed visit to the university.

Nicholas tore down the message and picked up the pen that sat next to the telephone. Underneath his cousin Nancy's note, he wrote *'Meeting with Mrs. Baines at Newham University, Wednesday 12th at 11.30am. Come if you want to. I want you to. Nicholas'.*

He left the note in the middle of the kitchen table and went off to find some food. He wished that Tracey Albourne was next to him. Nicholas really wished Tracey Albourne was next to him.

-0-

His cousin Nancy arrived back from her stay at his cousin Billy's late on Tuesday evening. Nicholas was in his bedroom when he heard a car pull up outside and the front door open and close. He listened to his cousin Nancy heave a deep sigh as she stepped lightly up the stairs. She closed her bedroom door and the house fell silent. Heavy eyed, Nicholas was about to fall asleep when he heard the welcome noise of his mobile telephone vibrating. Tracey Albourne. He grabbed the device from his bedside table.

There was a WhatsApp message.

'Hi ya Lovaboy it's me [heart shaped emoji] are ya awake [grinning face emoji] just got a sec whilst shes in the bathroom [thumbs up emoji] we are cummin home on sat [clapping hands emoji] I'll zoom over to your place [person on motorbike emoji]. Miss ya. [sad face emoji] See ya! [boy swimming emoji]. TA xxxxx [vibrating heart emoji]'.

Nicholas read it through five times. He felt an actual tear form in his left eye. Nicholas hurriedly wiped it away. He thought 'roll on Saturday'. But first he was meeting Mrs. Baines tomorrow, 11.30am Newham University.

All this pondering had made Nicholas tired.
Sapped, he fell asleep.

-0-

There was a tense and sullen atmosphere in his cousin Nancy's car as the pair made their way across to the university. Nicholas had fully expected to have to make his own way to his appointment, but just as he was about to leave, his cousin Nancy jangled her car keys in front of him and indicated with a nod of her head that she was going to go with him. She wasn't smiling. Her face mirrored a mixture of grimness and apprehension.

Much to Nicholas's relief, they arrived at 11.15 well in time for the appointment time, 11.30.

Nicholas liked punctuality.

Mrs. Baines welcomed Nicholas and his cousin Nancy into her office. There was a tray of cups and saucers with a large teapot steaming in the middle. Nicholas noticed a plate of digestive biscuits. He wondered how Mrs. Baines knew that tea and digestive biscuits were one of his favourite combinations.
Nicholas immediately started to like Mrs. Baines.
They all exchanged pleasantries and sipped tea. Nicholas nibbled on a biscuit. His cousin Nancy wore a stern frown. Mrs. Baines explained how the university worked and how they could offer Nicholas time to train and to study. As Nicholas had already successfully completed four of his GCSEs, he could combine the further six he planned to take here at the university and back at his school. Nicholas noticed that Mrs. Baines could see that his cousin Nancy was staring down at her cup of tea. She appeared not to be listening to Mrs. Baines. Seeing this, Mrs. Baines frowned at Nicholas, who responded with a small shrug of his shoulders.
Mrs. Baines suggested that they both join her to view the swimming facilities and their 'expensively built gymnasium'.

The pool was a still and deep blue. The gymnasium had every conceivable piece of apparatus.

Mrs. Baines looked proud.

Nicholas was impressed.

His cousin Nancy remained expressionless.

Nicholas had observed that, as the three of them walked through the wide corridors of the university, his cousin Nancy was taking time to examine pictures that hung on the walls. He saw that she would stop and stare at any image or words that depicted past and current university staff.

It was as if she was searching for someone in particular.

Nicholas wondered who she was looking for.

Back in Mrs. Baines's office, Mrs. Baines turned to Nicholas. She explained that she had entered him into the County Swimming Gala this coming Saturday as she wanted to see him 'first hand' in action. Nicholas wondered which one was her 'first hand'. He looked at Mrs. Baines's hands. She had a left one and a right one. He wondered which one she chose as her 'first hand'. He concluded that it was probably her right hand as he saw that she held her cup in her right hand. The County Swimming Gala was at the familiar Neptune Swimming Baths in the town. He thanked Mrs. Baines and told her that he was 'looking forward to it'.
Mrs. Baines nodded and then addressed his cousin Nancy. She said that with the lead up to the National Swimming Championships about to start there would almost certainly be some local media interest in Nicholas and possibly some national interest as well. She went on to say that if Nicholas stayed on the same upwards trajectory he could well be invited to train with other Olympic hopefuls. She said that if this happens, the national media definitely would want to know more about Nicholas.

Nicholas and Mrs. Baines were visibly shocked at his cousin Nancy's response.

She hesitated for a moment and then jumped up and stared directly at Mrs. Baines. She screamed, "NO... NO... NO... NO... THIS CAN'T HAPPEN... THIS HAS TO STOP... I WON'T ALLOW IT!"

His cousin Nancy grabbed her handbag. Her face was crimson in anger.

A startled Mrs. Baines tried to calm his cousin Nancy. She said quietly, "Don't worry; we'll make sure he is properly managed. We have a very professional PR team." Mrs. Baines tried to sound reassuring, but his cousin Nancy just glared fiercely at Mrs. Baines and marched out of the office, muttering some angry, incomprehensible words. She went straight to her car and drove out of the car park, leaving Nicholas and Mrs. Baines sitting, stunned, shocked and silent.

An astonished Mrs. Baines looked at a crestfallen Nicholas. "I'll give you a lift home."

-0-

This was supposed to be the best Saturday for Nicholas in a long time. Today was Tracey Albourne's homecoming and he was competing in the County Swimming Gala this afternoon. This was Nicholas's twin passions all rolled into a single twelve hours. Nicholas had texted Tracey Albourne telling her about the County Swimming Gala and that when he got home he would call her so that they could meet up.

She replied with a heart wrapped with bow emoji and a very smiley face emoji and arrow through a heart emoji.
So her mother Sharon is still restricting her using her phone, thought Nicholas.

Ever since his cousin Nancy's extraordinary outburst in Mrs. Baines's office, the past two days were the most difficult that Nicholas had previously endured. They had mostly avoided each other. Nicholas spent a large part of his time in his bedroom, even choosing to eat in there. His cousin Nancy busied herself in cleaning every conceivable item in the kitchen.

Today was the day of the County Swimming Gala. Nicholas had packed his swimming gear. He then unpacked it and repacked it. He slung his bag over his left shoulder and quietly slipped out of the front door. He headed for the bus stop.

His two races were soon over. He hadn't raced against these individuals previously, so he wasn't sure what to expect from them, but within three quarters of the first length he was already well ahead and finished both races comfortably and easily within himself.

As he stepped down from the top of the podium idly fingering a golden medallion that had been placed over his head by a balding man in a grey suit, Nicholas could hear shouting and screaming in the far corner of the pool near the exits. Everyone turned to see what was causing this commotion. He could see that two burly men were trying to restrain someone. He heard them say something like, "I don't care who you are... you can't enter the pool area. It's restricted. Please stand back."

There was some shouting and scuffling as the two men tried to hold on to a figure that was furiously trying to get away from their grasp.

Then he heard a familiar voice.

It was a very familiar voice.

The familiar voice shrieked, "Get your rotten hands off me," and with one loud shout, "NICHOLAS," the unmistakeable features of Tracey Albourne burst out between the two men. Pushing away their now feeble attempts to hold her back, she ran right up to Nicholas and grabbed the lapels of his white towelling robe. She planted a firm wet kiss on the centre of his bare chest.

"Missed me?"

"Yes," said Nicholas calmly. "Welcome back." He smoothed her long brown hair.

As Tracey Albourne buried her head deep into his chest, Nicholas looked over Tracey Albourne's head and spotted Mrs. Baines looking directly at him.

She was smiling.

Chapter 8. Nicholas and the Plan

It was 9.30 in the morning and Nicholas was still in bed. He was silently reliving his successes in both the freestyle and breaststroke disciplines in Saturday's County Swimming Gala. Following these achievements, Mrs. Baines, his new swimming coach and mentor, told Nicholas not to come into university. He was 'to take the day off to aid his recovery'. Her command puzzled Nicholas. He wasn't ill and therefore he hadn't got anything to recover from. In fact, he felt rather well, but Mrs. Baines wasn't the type of person to argue with, so he remained at home.

It had been a strange weekend for Nicholas, with the continuing strained atmosphere between him and his cousin Nancy, Nicholas had spent Saturday evening and most of Sunday at his girlfriend, Tracey Albourne's, house.

On Saturday evening Nicholas and Tracey Albourne sat side by side on the living room settee poring over his latest book on Greek Gods and Goddesses; *Greek Mythology: Myths and Legends of the Gods.* Tracey Albourne's mother Sharon was watching the BBC soap, Casualty. Every few minutes the couple looked up from the pages and turned to each other, spontaneously giggling. On the fourth giggle, her mother Sharon frowned and put the television on hold, insisting that they tell her 'what was so funny'.

After some prompting, Nicholas recounted an abbreviated version of her daughter's tussle with the security guards at the Neptune Pool and her slightly comical 'storming' the finalists' medal ceremony. Her mother Sharon looked up and shook her head muttering something that sounded like 'that's my Tracey; maybe they thought she was a terrorist or something'. She smiled slightly and went back to watching Casualty. The pair started giggling again, but a stern look from her mother Sharon cautioned them against continuing.

At ten o'clock Nicholas announced he was going home. He knew that his cousin Nancy always went to bed straight after Casualty, so he could slip in quietly and thus avoid any confrontation.

Relations between him and his cousin Nancy were at an all-time low. They mainly avoided each other and if they did find themselves inescapably in close proximity to each other they could barely muster a mutual silent nod. His cousin Nancy had still not explained her sudden and very voracious objection to Nicholas training and studying at Newham University. Stubbornly, Nicholas was not minded to ask.

Immediately after the ill-fated meeting, Nicholas had sent a brief text to Tracey Albourne outlining what was said. With Tracey Albourne now back from her holiday he had given her the full details. Tracey Albourne had listened in silent astonishment. When he had finished speaking, Nicholas was shocked at what she suggested he should tell his cousin Nancy to do to herself. An act Nicholas thought was actually physically impossible!

Sunday had been a good day for Nicholas. He was again at Tracey Albourne's house, arriving just after breakfast. He had spied his cousin Nancy eating hers in the conservatory, so he quietly slipped out of the front door.

Sunday was going to be far from a day of rest and relaxation. This Sunday had been chosen to be a day of complex calculation. To date, Tracey Albourne's academic accomplishments had been patchy, particularly in maths, whereas Nicholas's corresponding achievements had sent him soaring to the pinnacle of his class in many subjects. In most situations, Tracey Albourne liked to be on top, she didn't like being second best and currently, academically-wise, their relationship was definitely one-sided. She could feel Nicholas's influence coursing into her psyche, increasing her determination to 'level things up a bit' and she felt getting better results in her forthcoming examinations would be a good start. So, on Sunday, the pair put aside all thoughts about Greek Gods and Goddesses and settled down to work through her maths revision. They even refrained from kissing; an act they particularly enjoyed. This forbearance had demanded a huge effort by both parties, particularly as her mother Sharon had left them alone in the house for several hours whilst she gossiped with her neighbours.

After demolishing a plate of cheese sandwiches and swigging a bottle of Diet Coke, Nicholas shut Tracey Albourne's books with a smiling flourish, signalling an end to their session. He was satisfied that she was fit and ready for her maths examinations.

After saying their goodbyes, sealed with a rather long kiss (abstinence was now over), Nicholas set out on the short journey back to his house.

He sneaked in through the front door. Halfway up the stairs he felt his phone vibrate. It was a WhatsApp message from Tracey Albourne. She said she now had a 'ginormous headache'. This, according to her message, could only be soothed by a 'hot soapy bath and an early night'. But she concluded that she was now definitely 'up for it on Monday' and that 'she was going show that smart arse Libby Acton and her mate Louise Charlton just who was the Queen Bee when it came to doing sums'.

She added a heart emoji at the end.

Nicholas felt rather pleased with himself. He replied with a 'thumbs up' and 'vibrating heart' emoji.

As he readied himself for bed, he thought about his relationship with Tracey Albourne. He liked her 'happy-go-lucky' attitude towards life (which was in stark contrast to his own), but he was becoming aware that his own successes in both swimming and schoolwork could overshadow their relationship. He hoped that his help with her schoolwork would bring them closer together.
Just as Tracey Albourne was beginning to grace academia, Nicholas was starting to embrace empathy.

This was something that neither of them had previously considered.

-0-

Whilst Nicholas lay in bed 'recovering' and totally unbeknown to him, his cousin Nancy had arranged a meeting with Mrs. Baines by telephone that very Monday morning.

Precisely at noon the two women were sitting opposite each other in Mrs. Baines spacious office.

At 12.32, his cousin Nancy was slumped forward in her chair and had her hands covering her face with an alluvion of tears seeping through her fingers.

Mrs. Baines was looking stunned. Not knowing how to respond, she looked up at the painted portrait of a past Chancellor hanging on the office wall, as if she was trying to seek some inspiration from it. The aged, lined face with light blue eyes just stared blankly back at Mrs. Baines. As she turned her attention away, and just out of the corner of her eye, she swore that she saw a slight shrug of the shoulders from this past distinguished character.

The office was totally still and silent. It was almost as if someone had removed all the oxygen from the room and created a vacuum.

Finally, Mrs. Baines straightened up and pushed over a box of paper tissues towards her counterpart.

They both looked directly at each other.

Mrs. Baines spoke first. "And Nicholas doesn't remember anything about this?"

His cousin Nancy looked up and gently nodded, muttering, "Well, Nicholas was quite young when it happened, he seems to have forgotten all about it and as it's never mentioned within the family, we think that his mind has wiped away any memory of his past." His cousin Nancy hesitated adding, "At least we hope it has. He never asks about it," she added quietly.

Mrs. Baines stood up and walked slowly towards the window. She paused deep in thought. Nicholas had too much talent both academically and in swimming, she couldn't let these gifts go to waste. She wouldn't allow it. Turning, she informed his cousin Nancy that although she understood that any intrusive investigations into Nicholas's past could be extremely problematic for him and other members of the Davison family, they both needed to come up with 'a plan' that the two of them could put into place. "This plan," she continued, "would ensure that Nicholas reached his full potential, whilst keeping a tightly woven cloak over his past.

"Let's get to work," Mrs. Baines informed his cousin Nancy, staring at her eye to eye. "We need to do this for Nicholas." Nancy cast a doubtful eye at Mrs. Baines but nodded her agreement. Rising up, Mrs. Baines marched out of the office and ordered a tray of tea and biscuits. His cousin Nancy wiped her eyes dry.

-0-

Nicholas was sitting on the low school wall waiting for Tracey Albourne to come out of her maths examination. She had told him that the exam finished at 12.30. Nicholas looked at the time on his 'phone. It was now 12.46 and there was no sign of her. Nicholas started to get agitated. He checked his 'phone for messages. Maybe she was held up somewhere. He had estimated that if the exam finished at 12.30, it would take her seven minutes to gather up her books and pens, then three minutes to leave the school hall, so she should be outside at 12.43.

So, she was now three minutes late and there were no messages.

Nicholas didn't like lateness.

He was about to call her, when he heard her very distinctive laugh. Tracey Albourne appeared from the school main entrance alongside Louise Charlton and Mandy Johnson. The first thing that Nicholas noticed was that Mandy Johnson no longer needed to put grey socks in her bra, something that Tracey Albourne had accused her of doing when she was younger. He could clearly observe through her rather tight, white T shirt, that she had 'grown up' considerably! His thoughts made him blush a pale shade of pink.
Calming himself he could see that all three girls were in fits of giggles. Louise Charlton was actually doubled up in laughter and Tracey Albourne and Mandy Johnson had to hold her up.

Nicholas fired them a puzzled look.

The trio waved to him and skipped over to where he sat.
Mandy Johnson started talking, "You'll never guess what, Nick."
Nicholas winced, he hated being called 'Nick' – it reminded him of a police station and Nicholas didn't like the idea of being named after a police station. Also, there was something else that he couldn't quite put his finger on that made him shudder when someone called him Nick.

Mandy Johnson ignored his frown and continued speaking in a slightly squeaky voice. "The woman invigilator... well she... like... well she... you know... like... she let one off."

Cue fits of laughter from the three girls.

Nicholas looked mystified. He asked, "Let one what off?"

His reply just started off even more giggling.

Tracey Albourne composed herself and took a deep breath. She dabbed her eyes with the tissue that Nicholas had thoughtfully handed to her. She knew Nicholas well enough now that she would have to explain Mandy Johnson's words.

"A fart, Nicholas, you know a bottom burp."

"Yes," interrupted Louise Charlton, "us three were right at the front, we could hear it clearly." She wiped a tear from her eye on the back of her hand. Nicholas handed her a tissue.
"It sounded like a dog growling," added Louise Charlton.
"And it echoed around the hall," squeaked Mandy Johnson, laughing. She became the next recipient of a Nicholas tissue.
"She even looked behind her as if someone else had done it," said a chuckling Tracey Albourne who was now holding onto the wall for support.

All three were now patting their eyes with Nicholas's tissues, each taking deep breaths trying to calm themselves, Louise Charlton and Mandy Johnson were holding on to Nicholas's arms for support. Nicholas couldn't think what was remotely funny about breaking wind. He didn't do it often and certainly not when people were nearby, but it was just a natural bodily function – no big deal. But they obviously thought it was funny so he smiled in unison with the girls.

He quickly decided it was time to move onto a more important subject. "How was the exam?" he asked them. All three went silent, their smiles quickly dissipated.

"Er, well, it was okay," said Mandy Johnson. Nicholas noted that she didn't sound terribly convincing.

"Yeah, not too bad," replied Louise Charlton, who likewise appeared to Nicholas to be 'putting a brave face on'.

Nicholas looked across at Tracey Albourne. He wrinkled his brow in her direction. He detected a rather smug look on her face. She just mouthed one word to him.

"Easy."

Nicholas grinned.

-0-

Nicholas and Tracey Albourne decided to spend the rest of the afternoon in Preston Park eating ice cream.

They sat on their favourite park bench. She was nibbling on a white chocolate Magnum; he was sucking an orange ice lolly. Neither of them was speaking.

Tracey Albourne was the first to finish. She attentively licked the wooden stalk and when she was satisfied that it was completely clean on both sides, she looked up at Nicholas. She reached up her right hand to her mouth and scratched her top lip. Nicholas froze. He knew that when she did this an awkward question was about to hit him.

Tracey Albourne hesitated.
"Look, Nicholas, I know you don't like talking about your past, but surely you must want to know about your childhood and your parents, I mean it's only natural?"

Nicholas bit aggressively into his ice lolly. A swirling feeling started to unfurl in his insides. He tried to calm it.

He didn't feel natural.

He felt far from natural.
Tracey Albourne took his hand and held it tenderly. She lightly stroked his fingers. She looked at him directly in his eyes. A troubled look returned her gaze.

Nicholas fought hard against the whirling in his stomach. His mind pressed heavily against the firewall that was imbedded in his brain and was blocking anything and everything prior to the time he lived with his grandmother and grandfather.

Tracey Albourne said very gently, "You should ask your cousin Nancy."

Nicholas knew he should. He just didn't know why he couldn't.

But he just couldn't.

Tracey Albourne nestled her head deep into Nicholas's chest.
He heard her say, "God, I love you so much, Nicholas, but we must know. We have to know."

But Nicholas didn't want to know.

Chapter 9. Nicholas and Poseidon's Trident

Nicholas was upstairs in his bedroom sorting out his gym kit ready for his morning gym session at Newham University. As he assembled his T shirts, shorts, socks, underwear and trainers into his regular order, his ears pricked up. He could hear raised voices in the hallway.

It was two female voices.

It soon became apparent to Nicholas that his cousin Nancy and his girlfriend Tracey Albourne were having some sort of disagreement. Nicholas stopped his packing and crept quietly onto the landing. At the end of the hallway next to their front door he could see the large figure of his cousin Nancy aggressively pointing her index finger at Tracey Albourne, who in turn, with hands on her hips, was staring directly at her aggressor. Nicholas could see a wild, fixed stare in Tracey Albourne's eyes outfacing his cousin Nancy.
In their year-long relationship, Nicholas hadn't ever witnessed that look.

He inched forward and listened hard to their confrontation.

"It's nothing TO DO WITH YOU, young lady. I suggest that you keep your nose OUT OF OUR BUSINESS."

"But... it has lots to do with me. I'm, like, Nicholas's girlfriend... I NEED to know; Nicholas NEEDS TO KNOW."

"Yes, and I'm his cousin and guardian, it has NOTHING TO DO WITH YOU. I'M NOT GOING TO DISCUSS THIS ANYMORE so I suggest you leave... NOW."
The two women paused. Tracey Albourne spotted Nicholas crouched at the top of the stairs. He could see her face was filled with fury. Her eyes were glistening with angry tears. She looked up at him. "ASK HER," she shouted at him, pleading. "PLEASE just ASK her."

Nicholas knew exactly what Tracey Albourne was referring to. He could feel a familiar swirling feeling chasing around in his lower stomach. It felt like there was something real and alive in the pit of his insides. This unwelcome sensation was the same feeling he had whenever the subject of his past came out into the open. Nicholas fought hard against it. He looked down at the two women, who were both standing still and gazing up at him.

One pair of eyes was narrowed and intimidating. The other pair was wide and imploring.

Nicholas felt intimidated.

Nicholas didn't like feeling intimidated.

He pulled himself up, turned and fled back into his bedroom.
He heard Tracey Albourne cry out from the bottom of the stairs.
"I DON'T KNOW HOW YOU LIVE WITH THIS... BITCH... BUT YOU'RE BOTH HIDING SOMETHING FROM ME AND UNTIL I KNOW WHAT IT IS, WE'RE..."

Nicholas heard Tracey Albourne sob loudly. "... FINISHED."

The front door slammed shut.

Nicholas buried his head into his pillow. The swirling in his stomach started to subside. Was this the end of Phase Four of his life? The best phase in his entire life?

Nicholas was confused.
Nicholas hated confusion.

Around ten minutes after Tracey Albourne's dramatic departure, Nicholas heard a light tapping on his bedroom door. He hoped to see the slim bright figure of Tracey Albourne appear from behind the door, but much to his disappointment the large dark shape of his cousin Nancy filled the doorway. She was holding a mug. Nicholas smelled coffee and dragged himself up into a sitting position. She handed him the mug.

"I don't know what you see in her, Nicholas." His cousin Nancy was speaking softly. "I mean she has no right to pry. It's as if she thinks she owns you or something."

Nicholas ignored her and sipped the hot coffee.

He saw so much in Tracey Albourne. Much more than his cousin

Nancy could even begin to appreciate.

Firstly, there was what he saw with his actual eyes. He mentally and spontaneously listed them in no order of preference.
1. Long brown hair
2. Sparkling hazel eyes
3. Soft pale skin
4. Lips he liked to kiss
5. Tight denim jeans
6. Pink Nike trainers

Secondly, and significantly, his conscience 'saw' so much more in Tracey Albourne. He quickly made another list.
1. A friend
2. A companion
3. A motivator
4. A person to kiss
5. A hand to hold
6. But most importantly...

... a person that mostly understood him.

Nicholas politely thanked his cousin Nancy for the coffee. As she left the bedroom, she patted a light hand on his shoulder. It made him shudder. She closed the door behind her.

Nicholas picked up his phone.

There were no messages.

-0-

Nicholas felt hollow. He could physically feel that a part of him was missing. The empty space lay just above his stomach and deep into his ribcage. He knew exactly what would fill this empty space. Tracey Albourne.

But since she fled from his house ten days earlier, he hadn't heard anything from her. No messages, no calls, nothing. He had contemplated calling or messaging her but every time he went to press the send button something stopped him. After all, it was her that ran out on him, shouting 'We're finished'.

Nicholas didn't want to be 'finished'.

Nicholas missed Tracey Albourne.

Nicholas really missed Tracey Albourne.
In contrast, the mood between him and his cousin Nancy had thawed somewhat. The pair was now on relatively reasonable speaking terms and on occasions they even had their evening meal together. Nicholas sensed that his cousin Nancy was actually pleased that he was no longer seeing Tracey Albourne. Although she never came out and actually said it to him, he noticed that she avoided mentioning Tracey Albourne by name. It was as if his cousin Nancy had decided that Phase Five of Nicholas's life had started, and this new phase didn't include Tracey Albourne.

Another thing that was puzzling Nicholas was his cousin Nancy's frequent calls between her and his swimming coach, Mrs. Baines. After his cousin Nancy's uncharacteristic outburst during their first meeting, which culminated in her slightly melodramatic departure, Nicholas couldn't possibly imagine how the two women could begin communicating in a civilised manner. However, they now seemed to be interacting regularly. Nicholas immediately deduced that their conversations must be about him, as when his cousin Nancy took a call, which he assumed was from Mrs. Baines, she would immediately move away from him, slipping into the next room or the garden. Her actions made it obvious to him that he should be excluded from listening to any part of their talk.

Just as Nicholas believed that his life was stabilising and Phase Four was progressing along nicely, 'all this' was happening. At one low point he actually thought about Robin and wondered what he was doing now. He was comforted by the thought that he was probably defending some other poor youngster from pushing boys and spiteful girls.

Robin was good at that sort of thing.

-0-

Nicholas checked his phone. It was 9.00 in the morning and there were no messages. The number 42 bus had just dropped him off in the High Street and he was heading off to catch the number 53 bus that took him to Newham University. The morning journey across the town always irritated Nicholas as there was a gap between the two buses of precisely 32 minutes. But to add to his irritation the number 53 bus was nearly always late starting, meaning that the 32 minutes gap often stretched as far as 38 minutes, adding an annoying extra six minutes to his waiting time.

Nicholas arrived at the bus station. In an attempt to control his vexation, Nicholas closed his eyes and began drumming his fingers on the back of the wooden bench, mentally counting down the seconds. After just a couple of minutes, he felt the bench jolt as someone sat down next to him. He opened one eye. He spied a familiar figure.

"Hi, Nick."

Nicholas winced. 'Nick' was far from his favoured form of greeting. Both of his eyes were now open. Mandy Johnson, one of his ex-classmates and a friend of Tracey Albourne was addressing him. Nicholas saw that she was wearing a light grey hoodie, black skinny jeans and bright, white Nike trainers. A beige cloth shoulder bag was slung loosely over her left shoulder. She gave him a thin smile and carried on speaking. "Are you off to Uni? Swimming or studying?"

Nicholas turned to Mandy Johnson and quietly replied, "Both." There was a brief moment of silence between them, then she said, "I'm doing a bit of shopping." There was another pause. Nicholas checked the time; approximately 22 minutes until the number 53 bus would arrive.

"She's in bits you know."

Mandy Johnson saw the alarm in Nicholas's face.

She quickly replied, "Not LITERALLY, Nick. Don't be daft." Mandy Johnson rolled her eyes. "She's just sad. She just misses you, a lot." Nicholas placed his hand onto his stomach. The cavernous hollow feeling was still there. He felt that he could almost push his hand right into it.
Mandy Johnson continued speaking, "Look, I don't know exactly what went on between you two, I just know she, like, had some sort of row with your cousin Nancy, but Nick, she's desperate to make it up... to both of you."

Nicholas looked deep into the face of Mandy Johnson. He saw that she had sad eyes. He paused and then spoke softly. "Can you get her to come to Preston Park, tonight at six?"

Mandy Johnson's face immediately brightened, and she nodded enthusiastically. "Yes, I'm sure I can. Whereabouts do you, like, want to meet?"

Nicholas replied, "She'll know where."

Mandy Johnson leaned over and gave Nicholas a slight hug followed by a small kiss on his left cheek. It was a welcome hug and kiss, but Nicholas wished they had come from Tracey Albourne and not Mandy Johnson.

She got up and waved him goodbye.

Nicholas sighed and checked the time on his phone... 11 minutes and 32 seconds until the arrival of the number 53 bus. There were no messages.

-0-

Poseidon was the god of the sea, earthquakes and horses. Although he was officially one of the supreme gods of Mount Olympus, he spent most of his time in his watery domain.

The swimming pool at Newham University was Nicholas's watery domain.

When he was submerged in deep water, all the thoughts that ravaged his mind about the four phases of his life were cast aside. They were firmly locked deep within him, in a dark, impenetrable safe with the combination only known to him. In the water, he cast aside the very existence of his cousin Nancy, cousin Billy, the unidentified man with the black briefcase and the mysterious three coffins [two large, one small] he had so clearly seen at his grandmother's funeral. Everything and anything, real, imagined or associated with the first four phases of his life became dissolved in his crystal clear, chlorinated, liquid world. It was only when he was in the water that Nicholas felt he was truly free. Just like the packets of *'Free From'* foods he had seen in the supermarkets, Nicholas felt 'Free From' the cryptic, confusing and curious life he had inherited. When he evolved into his hero, Poseidon, the outside world became muffled, repressed and smothered as the soft waves splashed invitingly around his ears.

He rarely thought about coming first.

He would admit that he did get some gratuitous satisfaction when he was looking down on the other boys from the top of the podium. But Nicholas was more aware that his winning meant considerably more to the 'others': Mr. Braithwaite, Mr. Fahey [call me Joe] and now Mrs. Baines.

So, he did it for them.

But most of all he did it for Tracey Albourne.

-0-

Nicholas was towelling himself dry when he heard the sharp, clipped tones of Mrs. Baines from the other side of the door. She was asking him to 'pop by' her office for a 'quick chat' before he left to go home. Nicholas always thought that the phrase 'pop by' was a curious one. To Nicholas a 'pop' was that funny noise you made when you stuck you finger into the side of your mouth and flicked it out quickly. Or something fizzy you drank. Or even a weird name for your father. Nicholas wasn't sure how to 'pop by' her office, so he resolved to quickly get dressed and simply knock on her door and say 'Hi'.

Mrs. Baines was standing in front of her oak desk when Nicholas 'popped' his head around the office door. She invited him with a generous smile. She complimented him on his recent efforts and said he had been 'working hard'. She added that in the next session they were going to work on his 'starts and turns' as in the longer disciplines a 'good turn' can 'gain a few vital centimetres' on his opponents.

Nicholas nodded in agreement. Nicholas always nodded in agreement with Mrs. Baines. He respected her knowledge. She was much more subtle in her approach to coaching him than Mr. Fahey [call me Joe] had been. Nicholas had never heard her say 'hit the water 'aard' once.

Nicholas noticed that Mrs. Baines had now changed her expression to a more serious one. Her mouth was pursed and her eyes hardened. He saw that she rubbed her hands together as if she was trying to warm them up. Nicholas thought that this was weird as it was already quite hot in her office. Mrs. Baines spoke quietly. She said that she and her team were 'right behind him'. Nicholas looked over his shoulder. There wasn't a 'team' behind him, just an oak panelled door. He turned back to Mrs. Baines, who was now smiling. She said she didn't mean it 'figuratively', she just wanted him to know that she and the rest of Newham University swimming coaching people were going to look after him and keep him away from the 'limelight'. Nicholas remembered being taught about 'lime-lights' in his drama lessons (which he hated) at school. A 'limelight' was a lamp with a flame directed at a cylinder of lime with a lens to concentrate the light and they were rarely used on stage these days. Nicholas thought that he would be quite happy to stay away from the limelight as he recalled that they looked quite dangerous.

But Nicholas didn't want this conversation to drag on. He needed to catch the number 53 bus into town and then walk to Preston Park for six o'clock. The number 53 bus left in ten minutes, so he thanked Mrs. Baines saying he would see her 'in a couple of days' and not to worry about 'lime-lights', he would avoid them at 'all costs'. Nicholas then turned the shiny brass handle on the big oak door and stepped into the corridor that led to the front of the university.

Mrs. Baines shook her head and took a large sip of water from the glass tumbler that sat on her desk. As Nicholas left Mrs. Baines's office he heard her release a large sigh.
Once outside, Nicholas trotted to the bus stop.

-O-

Nicholas arrived at Preston Park at exactly 5.58. He headed straight for their favourite park bench. As he approached the bench, he was relieved to spot a familiar figure sitting at the far end of the bench.

Nicholas sat down at the other end.

Neither spoke.

Suddenly, the familiar figure leaned down and picked up a curiously shaped parcel.

She handed it to Nicholas.

"I've brought you a present. Open it."

Nicholas tore at the fancy wrapping paper and pulled out his gift. He nearly collapsed in laughter.

There, in his hand, was a three-pronged fork with a long metal handle with a sharp spike at the end. It was undoubtedly Poseidon's Trident – the 'Earth Shaker'.

The stem was engraved *'from your own Aphrodite, TA'*.
Nicholas grabbed the handle and playfully poked Tracey Albourne in the ribs. Laughing, she made vain attempts to fend him off. He stood up in front of her and waved the Trident over his head shouting,

"I Am Poseidon!
God of the Sea!
I swim at Newham University!"

They both fell into each other's arms, laughing and crying in equal proportions. Nicholas had one hand gripped tightly around Tracey Albourne's waist, in his other, he held Poseidon's Trident in a victory salute above their heads.
After a few minutes they fell quiet.

"You called my cousin Nancy a horrible name."

Tracey Albourne looked down and nodded gently. "That's why I just couldn't call you, I was worried that I'd gone too far and really upset you. I shouldn't have called her that. I am really sorry." After a few moments of silence, she glanced up and with an impish look she said quietly, "... and she doesn't look anything like a female dog, I mean she's got two legs and not four, nor does she have a tail or a wet nose..."

Nicholas knew she was making fun of him.

Nicholas liked Tracey Albourne making fun of him.

Nicholas said softly, "She does have a rather long pink tongue though..."

The couple burst out into a fit of giggles.

Nicholas put his Trident down on the bench and assumed what he hoped was his 'serious face'.

"You've got to make it up to her or we are going to have a very rough time of it."

Tracey nodded replying, "I know, and I will." She added quickly, "So are we back together again?"

Nicholas thought for a second. He lifted his Trident and tapped Tracey Albourne gently on the top of her head with the middle fork.

"We were never apart."

Chapter 10. Nicholas and Dr. J. Hazel

Nicholas was annoyed.

Nicholas didn't like being annoyed.

He was packing his books away at the end of his applied mathematics lesson, when he felt his phone vibrate in his trouser pocket. He studiously waited until he left the classroom and was outside before he checked his phone for messages.

There was just one.

It read: *'Gym and pool closed all day – unforeseen circumstances – will update you tomorrow – Mrs. B.'*

Nicholas read the message twice, he then rather aggressively clicked delete and rammed the phone deep into his trouser pocket. He didn't like having his plans altered at the last moment. Yesterday evening, in his customary style, Nicholas had mapped out his timetable for the following day. His plans started with school in the morning - a double applied mathematics lesson - then a swift walk into town to catch the number 53 bus to Newham University. Lunch would be in the university canteen. After his accustomed 'Thursday' meal, comprising of a toasted cheese sandwich with a carton of orange juice, he had intended to have a strong workout in the university gym followed by an uninterrupted minimum forty lengths of the pool - twenty front crawl and twenty breaststrokes. But now, because of 'unforeseen circumstances' he was going to have make alterations to his schedule and Nicholas found this all very disconcerting.

With a deep sigh he sat down on the low wall that circled the school and pondered his next move.
His first thought was to message his girlfriend, Tracey Albourne, but he quickly remembered that she was on a school visit to the Globe Theatre in London as part of her drama group.

Nicholas had encouraged her to take up drama.

With a common interest in Greek Gods and Goddesses they had decided to write and then enact their own private performance centred upon the love affair between Poseidon (Nicholas) and Aphrodite (Tracey Albourne). It was a full costume event and set to be played out in the privacy of Tracey Albourne's bedroom when her mother Sharon was out on a date with her latest boyfriend. According to Tracey Albourne, her mother Sharon had managed to find 'yet another loser'. But, at precisely 7.30 in the evening, they were both delighted to see her mother Sharon step in Mr. Hussain's taxi all dressed up for her date. As the car disappeared down the street, they dashed upstairs and quickly changed into their respective costumes.

At the end of the evening the pair deemed their first rendition to be an 'Oscar winning performance'. They both agreed that they would try to re-enact their Poseidon/Aphrodite affair as often as possible! It was the next day and over lunch in the school canteen that Nicholas suggested to her that she should join the newly formed school drama and theatre group. He had seen a poster advertising it on the school noticeboard. Tracey Albourne agreed to give it a try. That same afternoon she had been keenly and warmly embraced by the group and much to Nicholas's satisfaction she said that she had 'such a fun time' that she had immediately enrolled herself in for the remainder of the term.
Nicholas was delighted that Tracey Albourne had taken up amateur acting, but now he had more pressing things to consider. Namely what was he going to do with his unpremeditated free afternoon? So, he pushed Tracey Albourne's drama exploits to one side, and with a wry smile, he tucked away all sentiments relating to the activities of their alter egos, Poseidon and Aphrodite, and concentrated on what to do next.

He checked the time on his phone. It was now just after twelve noon. He observed that a small trickle of students were exiting the school buildings and had begun gathering together in close, conspiratorial clumps.

This signalled that it was time for him to move on. He considered heading off to his local swimming pool; the Neptune Baths. But he quickly rubbed this thought out, remembering that Thursday afternoon at the Neptune Baths was 'The Pensioner PM Club' and people of his age were not welcomed. Besides, the thought of witnessing masses of semi-naked wrinkly bodies did not appeal to Nicholas.

Nicholas slowly levered himself up from the wall and decided to head home. He remembered that his cousin Nancy had been shopping yesterday, so quite possibly the cupboards, fridge and freezer would likely be full of goodies. His cousin Nancy had quite a sweet tooth and she wasn't shy at filling up the kitchen with an assortment of biscuits, cakes and puddings. She also regularly stocked up with lager and beer.

As he reluctantly trudged the short journey homewards, he mused over the state of the relationship between Tracey Albourne and his cousin Nancy. Despite a recent rather savage altercation, they now appeared to have called a truce. Nicholas wasn't party to their 'peace talks' and he didn't ask what was discussed, but he was relieved to observe that they were now on relatively civil terms. Nicholas's thoughts abruptly returned to the present day as he arrived at his house. He was surprised to see that there were two cars parked in his driveway. He recognised them both. One was his cousin Nancy's slightly battered blue Ka and the other was his cousin Billy's pristinely polished, Ford Mondeo.

Nicholas was confused.

Nicholas didn't profess to know his cousin Billy intimately, but he was well aware that his cousin Billy was not noted for his spontaneity. This led Nicholas to judge that this must be an arranged visit.

Nicholas mischievously leaned against the passenger door of cousin Billy's shiny car. He immediately spied another car parked outside of his house that he didn't recognise. Nicholas knew all his neighbours' cars individually and this wasn't one that was normally stationed here. He lifted himself away from his cousin Billy's car and approached the mystery car. He bent down and looked inside. The back seat was empty so he turned his attention to the front passenger seat. Intermingled between a pair of brown leather gloves was a blue lanyard with a name badge attached to it. It looked very similar to the name badges that visitors to his school wore. Nicholas peered deep into the car trying to read the name and details on the badge.

He could clearly interpret, 'Dr. J. Hazel – Consultant Psychiatrist'. He couldn't quite make out where Dr. J. Hazel did his psychiatry as one of the fingers of the glove was obscuring the centre of the text. It read 'Ram... something... 'pital'. He could see a partially concealed NHS logo on the top right-hand corner of the badge. Nicholas presumed that the last five letters referred to an NHS hospital. He pulled out his phone and took a picture of the badge.
Nicholas paused for a moment and absentmindedly rubbed his chin. It was obvious that this Dr. J. Hazel was visiting his house but why was he here? Two thoughts flashed through his mind. Was his cousin Nancy mentally ill? He hadn't seen any signs. Did his cousin Billy have mental health issues? His cousin Billy always seemed permanently morose, but Nicholas didn't consider that constituted a 'mental health' matter.

Nicholas was puzzled.

Nicholas didn't like being puzzled.

He straightened himself up. A familiar feeling started rise in the pit of his stomach. As this unwelcome sensation slowly revealed itself, Nicholas became convinced that this meeting wasn't anything to do with his cousins' mental health conditions, but it was him that was in some way connected to this gathering.

Nicholas crouched down between the two cars and like a soldier hiding from a sniper he crept quietly up the side of his house. He guessed that if there was a meeting it was likely to be held in the conservatory as this was his cousin Nancy's favourite room. It was light and airy and furnished with three generously proportioned paisley patterned armchairs.

Nicholas had thought correctly. He could clearly hear the murmuring of adult voices coming from the partially opened conservatory window. He stilled. They were talking conversationally. It was obvious that they weren't expecting to be overheard. He leaned forward to listen. The first voice he recognised was his cousin Nancy's.

She was saying," … Look, I'm not sure how long I can keep a lid on this… SHE's meddling … that so-called girlfriend of his… and then there's the Uni… someone's going to put two and two together… it'll all come out…"
Nicholas heard a cough and a grunt, which he discerned had come from his cousin Billy. There was a moment's silence. Nicholas softly raised himself and peered into the conservatory. All three armchairs were filled. The chairs had been arranged in a circle. His cousin Nancy was faced by his cousin Billy and an unfamiliar man sporting a trim grey beard and thick black framed spectacles. Each of them was holding a cup and saucer.

The best china, thought Nicholas rather incongruously.

The bearded man put his cup and saucer down onto a table positioned in the centre. Nicholas saw him rub his beard. He spoke quite softly. Nicholas pushed his ear forward and strained hard to hear him.
"… I'm confident that I can keep Janet in the dark… access to the news is heavily restricted … with the change in names… she probably won't get it anyway… she's…" Nicholas couldn't hear the last few words.

Nicholas heard his cousin Billy's gruff voice. Again, Nicholas struggled to hear him clearly. "... is Janet ... haven't visited her recently...is she..."

The bearded man nodded and frowned at his cousin Billy. Nicholas distinctly heard him say, "The same ... no real improvements." He paused. "But she does enjoy your visits."

His cousin Billy stared into his cup and then took a small sip. Nicholas saw him dip his head in a silent nod and rub his chin. Suddenly his cousin Nancy stood up and set her cup and saucer down on the arm of her chair. Nicholas heard her speak distinctively, "Oh, look at the time... table booked for one... we'll go in separate cars... we'll continue this over lunch..."

"Great," Nicholas heard his cousin Billy growl, "I'm starving."

All three stood up in unison.

Nicholas ducked down and stayed very still. He listened as the front door was slammed shut and then he heard three cars being driven away.

The sensation in Nicholas's stomach died away.

-0-

Nicholas and Tracey Albourne were sitting in Preston Park. It was a bright cool evening. Tracey Albourne was recounting her visit to the Globe, enthusiastically telling Nicholas all about William Shakespeare and his many plays. Nicholas listened diligently, but deep down he was aching to tell her about his own experiences and the encounter with his cousin Nancy, cousin Billy and a mystery bespectacled, bearded consultant psychiatrist, who he believed to be a Dr. J. Hazel.

Nicholas waited patiently for her to finish. Finally, she asked him,

"How was your day?"

Nicholas told her about the meeting in the conservatory. "There's something going on here… and it's got a lot to do with you." Tracey Albourne immediately admonished herself for saying something so blindingly obvious.

Nicholas pulled out his phone and showed her the picture of the identity badge bearing the name Dr. J. Hazel. Tracey Albourne immediately suggested that they Googled his name.

Google quickly obliged. *'Dr. Jonathan Hazel is an outstanding clinician with considerable expertise in forensic psychiatry. Dr. J. Hazel has worked at Rampton since January as a consultant and prior to this has worked in a number of NHS trusts, including the South London and the Peacock NHS Foundation Trust.'*

Nicholas and Tracey Albourne looked at each other in amazement. Nicholas spoke first. "Rampton, isn't that a place for locking up mad killers?"

Tracey Albourne shrugged and then Googled Rampton. Google announced, 'RAMPTON SECURE HOSPITAL is a high security psychiatric hospital near the village of Woodbeck between Retford and Rampton in Nottinghamshire, England.'

There was a long silence between the couple. They simultaneously stared across Preston Park Lake, both deep in thought. The water rippled and the setting sun's reflection twinkled across the lake.

Only the frantic quacking of a faraway duck interrupted the still quietness.

It was Tracey Albourne that broke the hush.

"We really HAVE to get to the bottom of this."

Nicholas nodded gently in reluctant agreement.

His stomach began to swirl.

"It's all about Phase One," he muttered.

Chapter 11. Nicholas and Eden Crematorium

Nicholas and Tracey Albourne were lying side by side on blue and red striped sun loungers located on the patio of Nicholas's house. It was a glorious summer's afternoon and the pair had sneaked away early from school.

Nicholas was shirtless and wearing blue knee-length shorts whilst Tracey Albourne had on her red and white spotted bikini top and tight red shorts. Both were sporting dark sunglasses which they hoped made them look 'cool'. The air around them was heavy in factor 30 sun cream that they had sensibly and liberally applied to all of their exposed skin.

But Nicholas was feeling guilty. Skipping school made him uncomfortable. Nevertheless, Tracey Albourne had been insistent, saying 'come on, Nicholas, it's only one bloody afternoon, we're in our last year and you can catch up with your work tomorrow. Besides, no one will miss us.'

Nicholas's guiltiness dissipated rapidly when Tracey Albourne appeared from his cousin Nancy's kitchen clutching two cans of Red Stripe. Tiny droplets of water ran invitingly down each can as the cold beer hit the warm air. Nicholas frowned, asking, "Aren't those my cousin Nancy's?"

Tracey Albourne rolled her eyes, muttering, "Chill, Nicholas, she won't notice, there's enough cans in the fridge to drown a drunk. She likes a drink does your cousin Nancy, doesn't she?"

Nicholas nodded in agreement. His cousin Nancy really did enjoy her 'juice'.

It was his devouring of the contents of the can that had encouraged Nicholas to finally open up to Tracey Albourne about his 'visions' at his grandmother's funeral. That disturbing experience had remained indelibly set in his mind and regularly resurfaced when his thoughts turned to his life in Phase One. He had made a tentative agreement with Tracey Albourne that she could gently push him to delve deep into his memory with an aim to slowly unlock the mystery of his early childhood. At times, the tightly constructed firewall blocking out Phase One showed signs of being infected with malware bytes which opened up small windows of opportunity to download snippets of Nicholas's past. Tracey Albourne's mild interrogations, using very carefully chosen words, were slowly burning into the fog that purled around the firewall and through Nicholas's brain.

As each anamnesis was uncovered it was accompanied by the strange, disturbing feeling that emanated from the pit of Nicholas's stomach and sometimes reached as high as his chest.

The combination of Tracey Albourne's soft probing and Nicholas's newfound, but still slightly reluctant, firmness of purpose to mentally uncover his past had unveiled three memories:

1. He could recall that as a young child he had lived with his mother and father, but their features and names failed to materialise.

2. He knew that his father had taken him swimming regularly and that Nicholas always wore the same blue swimming shorts that had two round badges sewn onto them.

3. Finally, he remembered that his mother often had long absences from home, but where she went remained a mystery.

Throughout their relationship, Tracey Albourne often had to adjust her unambiguous attitude towards life and align her own inclinations with the perplexities of Nicholas's own outlook. But, even with her recently acquired psychological skills, this afternoon's revelations about the three coffins he was absolutely adamant that he had witnessed at his grandmother's funeral, momentarily pressed her into an uncharacteristic, stunned silence.

Recovering, she pulled herself up and rested her chin in her hands repeating, "Say that again, I mean, like you DID see them? With your own eyes? Really? All THREE of them?"

Nicholas removed his sunglasses and stared intently at his navel, his fingers idly twiddling with the dark hairs growing in the centre of his chest. "Yes," he replied softly, "absolutely definitely. I'm not making this up."

The couple simultaneously laid back in silence. Ten quiet minutes passed. The bright sun beamed down on them. Nicholas could hear a bird urgently chirping in the trees, singing out a warning to his fellow feathered friends about an unknown danger. He rolled onto his side and gazed at Tracey Albourne. Even though her sunglasses covered a large proportion of her face, Nicholas instinctively recognised the look on her face. She was hatching a plan. Nicholas braced himself. Tracey Albourne's plans nearly always included him. In an attempt to thwart her machinations, he leaned over and kissed her gently on the lips. She pulled him close. "Can you remember where this funeral place was? Let's pay it a visit, we might just uncover something."

Nicholas sighed. His stomach started to roll. He could easily remember where it was. He was sure that he had been there at least twice before.

-0-

Tracey Albourne and her mother Sharon were in the kitchen and deep in conversation when they heard their front door being aggressively pushed open, followed by a loud strangulated shout that sounded like 'YOULLNEVERGUESSWHAT'. Startled, they both quickly put down their coffee mugs and ran into the hall. They were challenged by a red-faced, panting Nicholas waving his mobile phone over his head. Before they could confront him, the wide-eyed pair heard him gasp, "I'm in... (huff)... England."

Tracey Albourne grabbed his arm and steered the still blowing Nicholas into the kitchen. Her mother Sharon poured him a glass of water and ordered him to sit down and take a drink.

Nicholas sipped the water and started to take deep breaths.

Calmed, he handed his phone over to Tracey Albourne. He pointed at the screen. "Read it," he puffed. She read a text message. *'conrgats N you've been selected for the England squad, freestyle, home nation championships. I'll let you know more when you come to uni tomorrow. mrs B.'* She had added a smiley face emoji. Instantly, Tracey Albourne flung her arms around Nicholas and kissed him repeatedly on his face. Her mother Sharon initially pursed her lips at her daughter's naked display of affection, but eventually broke into a wide smile and patted a congratulatory hand on Nicholas's shoulder.

Tracey Albourne whispered in his ear calling him a 'hero'. Nicholas smiled. It reminded him of the time, now way back in their past, when she had described him as a 'hero' after the Junior Inter-Schools Swimming Championship. Nicholas always considered that encounter was the start of their journey together.

Tracey Albourne pulled away, "Have you told your cousin Nancy?" Nicholas stilled and slowly shook his head. "Not yet, I came straight round here."

Nicholas momentarily looked slightly guilty. He bit his bottom lip. Tracey Albourne and her mother frowned at him in unison. Nicholas got their message. He squeezed Tracey Albourne's hand and waved at her mother Sharon. "I'll go straight round now. Sorry." The two women ushered him down the hall and through the still open front door.

"Oh, and well done again," they shouted together. Closing the door behind them, they turned to each other and simultaneously burst out laughing.

"He's a rare one, that fella of yours," declared her mother, Sharon. A grinning Tracey Albourne agreed. "Unique."

-0-

Nicholas jogged the short distance from Tracey Albourne's house to his own home. Outside, he fumbled inside his short's pockets seeking out his front door key.

"Blast," he said to himself as he felt his wallet, phone and some loose coins, but no keys. He tapped on the front door and waited. Noting that his cousin Nancy's car was parked in the drive, he resolved that she must be in.

She's probably out the back, thought Nicholas and he slipped around the house and down the side.
His cousin Nancy was indeed 'out the back'. She was in the conservatory and she had company. Nicholas peered through the glass and into the room. His cousin Nancy was accompanied by the familiar, black briefcase carrying man. Nicholas had encountered the same man at his house on a couple of previous occasions.

Nicholas hesitated before he attracted his cousin Nancy's attention. He could see that she was writing something at the bottom of a typewritten A4 piece of paper. The man with the black briefcase was neatly assembling an array of papers and placing them inside his black case.

But Nicholas was spotted. His cousin Nancy and the black briefcase man glanced up and saw Nicholas standing at the window. Nicholas watched as his cousin Nancy hastily stuffed the paper she was writing on into a brown envelope and then thrust it furtively into the top drawer of their sideboard. She then waved him around to the rear of the conservatory and sprang up to open the door. The black briefcase man quickly rose and waved at Nicholas. He heard him muttering something like, 'Nice to see you again, young man, must dash, duty calls and all that'. In a flash, he was down the hallway and through the front door before Nicholas could respond.

-0-

Nicholas was in his bedroom working through his much-practised routine of assembling his swimming gear ready for the next day's session at Newham University. He would be under the guidance of his coach Mrs. Baines.

His cousin Nancy had remained decidedly downbeat about his swimming exploits, she rarely mentioned them and when she did, there was a distinct lack of interest on her behalf. Unsurprisingly, her reaction to Nicholas's latest news had been in complete contrast to the very enthusiastic response he had received from Tracey Albourne and her mother Sharon. She said words like 'don't get your hopes up' and 'you're only in the squad' plus 'you might not get picked'. But she did offer him a glass of sparkling wine by way of celebration, which they both enjoyed over supper.

As he concentrated on folding his clothes, Nicholas suddenly remembered that it was Tuesday and every Tuesday evening his cousin Nancy went to the local pub to 'meet with friends'.

That meant Nicholas was alone in the house.

He had an idea.

He left his bedroom and tiptoed quietly downstairs. He smiled to himself and stopped. Speaking out loud, he said, "Why am I tiptoeing? There's nobody here apart from me." He echoed the words that Tracey Albourne had said to him on so many occasions, "Nicholas you really are weird at times."

Nicholas entered the conservatory and headed straight for the sideboard. He pulled open the top drawer. The brown envelope that his cousin Nancy had earlier slipped into the drawer remained in place.

Nicholas pulled it out. Thankfully it was unsealed, so he reached inside and laid out the contents on the coffee table.

It was entitled 'LASTING POWER OF ATTORNEY – on behalf of JANET WISEMAN. The following text looked to Nicholas like legal jargon which he found confusing. However, he could see that it detailed his cousin Nancy's full name – Nancy Jane Davison and what he assumed was his cousin Billy's full title – William Albert Wiseman. Nicholas ran upstairs and grabbed his phone. He returned to the conservatory and took three pictures of the paper, then quickly returned it to the envelope and subsequently back into the drawer. Nicholas pondered. *Is this Janet the wife of my cousin Billy?* He hadn't heard of a wife being mentioned previously and if she was, why was his cousin Nancy involved?

She'll be keen to see this, thought Nicholas. *Detective Inspector Tracey Albourne will soon be on the case.*

-0-

Nicholas pulled the duvet tight over him. The time was 10.37. He heard the front door close and his cousin Nancy clamber noisily upstairs. He could hear her singing. It sounded like 'Single Ladies', by Beyoncé. Nicholas grinned.

He set his alarm for 5.00am and turned off the lamp.

-0-

Eden Crematorium was a short bus ride from the High Street. During their journey, Nicholas and Tracey Albourne briefly discussed Nicholas's recent discovery of his cousin Nancy's legal document. They both decided to put it to one side whilst they pursued the origins of his 'visions'. They alighted and walked hand in hand towards the main entrance. Tracey Albourne felt Nicholas's hand grow increasing moist as they entered the grounds. Nicholas wasn't surprised to feel the swirl in his stomach, he was expecting it.

The crematorium gardens were adorned with elegant figurines: small posies of flowers and white marble tributes. On the far side the couple spied a wall where names of the deceased were faithfully remembered. Tracey Albourne felt Nicholas stiffen. She could see that his eyes remained fixed firmly in front of him as if he was trying to avoid looking at the building. She slipped her arm around his waist, hoping that this would reassure him, and whispered in his ear," Let's look at those names over there. If you really did see two large coffins and one small, it seems logical to me that it's likely to be two parents and a child." Nicholas's face turned sour. Tracey Albourne tugged his waist.

She carried on speaking in low solemn tones. "You start at that end and I'll start here. Remember look for names that indicate two adults and a child all cremated at the same time. Shout if you see something interesting."

The couple split apart and silently began their quest.

Chapter 12. Nicholas and Tracey Albourne's HGV

As the white and grey coach slipped down Preston Park Hill, Tracey Albourne turned away and pulled down the zip on her hoodie. She needed air. She held onto the warm stone wall that surrounded the park and took several short shallow inhalations. As she started to recover, she felt a light tap on her elbow.

An elderly woman was looking up at her quizzically. "Are you all right, dear?" The woman spoke with concern.

Tracey Albourne nodded and forced a weak smile. "Yes, I'm fine, I've just seen my boyfriend leave for a ten-day swimming training camp. I'm just being a bit daft. Thanks. Sorry."

The lady nodded knowingly and gently smiled. "He'll be back before you know it."

But it wasn't the return of Nicholas that was troubling her.

It was;
Horrific
Gory
Vile

-0-

Tracey Albourne had learned about Nicholas's call-up to the Spain training camp through a short text message he received as they were on the bus returning home from their visit to Eden Crematorium. It would be an intensive coaching for ten days in the Spanish sunshine. The text included the phrase, 'The use of mobiles will be strictly limited'.

Nicholas had told her that he had decided that their trip to the crematorium had been a total failure. As far as he was concerned, they hadn't detected anything that may have caused his 'vision' of three coffins (two large, one small), that he had distinctively 'seen' at his grandmother's funeral.

But Tracey Albourne knew differently.

She sat quietly, gently holding on to Nicholas's arm reflecting on the past hour they had just spent in the crematorium grounds.

They had been looking through memorial plaques. The pair of them was searching for three names that would suggest that two adults and one child had been cremated together. The weather was hot and Tracey was beginning to tire. Her mouth was dry and her head felt it was going to burst. Every name she read was a life no longer; someone's father, mother, brother, sister, a child, a friend; all gone. She stopped and glanced across the grounds. She watched as Nicholas busily inspected each memorial with his trademark diligence. He was tracing his finger over each name and closely examining every tribute. As he worked his way down, the thought of her never seeing Nicholas again suddenly sprang, unwanted and uninvited, into her head. She immediately pushed it to the farthest corner of her mind and covered it with the thickest blanket she could muster and then pushed on with her task in hand.

She was nearing the end of the wall when a grey stone plaque with black lettering caught her attention. It read, *'In loving memory of Gary Wiseman – father, son, brother, friend and educator'*. *Wiseman*, thought Tracey Albourne. *That name is familiar.* Directly underneath was another similarly lettered plaque. Tracey Albourne had to stoop down to read it. *'There are so many special memories of Elaine Morse and her beloved daughter Brooke ~ both taken so tragically early.'* The plaque confirmed that the dates of all three deaths and their subsequent funerals were all identical. She let out a gasp.

It was the name 'Wiseman' that had been the trigger. Nicholas's cousin Billy was a Wiseman (in name only though, she thought) and Nicholas had mentioned that the legal document he had seen his cousin Nancy sign, also referred to a Janet Wiseman.

Tracey Albourne wiped her glistening brow with the sleeve of her jacket. She looked across the crematorium grounds and spied Nicholas nearing the end of his line of plaques. She quickly photographed the Wiseman memorial several times and downloaded copies onto her laptop via iCloud. Nicholas was now walking casually towards her slowly shaking his head. Tracey Albourne grimaced back in agreement. Something, deep inside her, whispered, 'not now.' Tracey Albourne listened and obeyed.

-0-

Three words leapt from her tablet screen. They danced aggressively in front of her eyes and then buried themselves deep into her brain.

Horrific
Gory
Vile

She steadied herself and scrolled to the top of the news report for a third time. Her hands clenched the sides of her tablet so fiercely she almost cracked the screen. A deluge of tears dripped unabated down each cheek. In just a few short sentences, she had gone from shock to revulsion and finally to sadness.

She placed her tablet onto the dining room table and pushed it away as if it had become infected with a disease. Her thoughts immediately turned to Nicholas. She could now so clearly understand why his family wanted to suppress all talk about his early life. She thought about his quirkiness and his attitude towards life. Was it his way of finding order in the chaos?

And why he hated being called Nick.

Her thoughts were interrupted as her phone started to vibrate and the screen lit up.

'Hi Trace. Just finished my first sesh. [swimming man emoji] All good. Went well. [thumbs up emoji] Weather down here is great. [sunshine emoji] The captain is a bit of a tyrant. He never smiles. [droopy mouth face emoji] Gonna go out for a meal in the town inabit. Missing you. Will call when I can. Byeeeeee! N. [heart shaped emoji]'

Tracey Albourne wiped her eyes dry and gently reapplied some eyeliner. She read the message twice. Her eyes started to fill up.

'Great. Missing you loads. [face with tears emoji]. Call me soon [telephone emoji]. Don't go off with any Dusky Senoritas [winky face emoji]. Stay safe. TA. [Heart shaped emoji].

-0-

"Don't take any notice of her… she's just pining for her Nicholas." Mandy Johnson was talking. She was surrounded by three other young women, Libby Acton, Louise Charlton and a sullen Tracey Albourne. A large jug of iced lemonade sat between them. "Come on, Trace, he'll back next week, for flip's sake, just cheer up." Tracey raised a flimsy smile and poured herself a drink. "Sorry, girls, it's just that I've got a bit on my mind at the moment."
Louise took a deep sip from her glass. 'Ooo do tell. Are you and everyone's favourite swimming champion, like, going through another rough patch? Come on, Trace, you can tell us, we're your friends."

Tracey Albourne flicked a piercing glance in Louise's direction.

"Nope, it's nothing like that, it's just … well, you know, this and that. Ignore me." Tracey Albourne wanted to change the subject, "Anyway, are you still going out with that Felix fella? The one with the big black motorbike?"

Louise nodded and laughed. "Here, come round a bit closer; I've got something to tell you about him. You'll laugh at this." She hesitated and looked across at Tracey Albourne, "Even you, Trace, this might cheer you up a bit."

They all leaned forward conspiratorially. Louise started to tell her story.

"He got into bed with your mother! How come?" exclaimed Mandy. "Yeah," confirmed Louise. "We came back to mine from the park last Friday where we had both been smoking some really good weed and we were a bit blazed. By the amount of empty wine bottles that greeted our return, it wasn't rocket science to work out that Mum had almost certainly gone to bed pissed. So, we both guessed that she would be dead to the world. I said to Felix, give it ten/fifteen minutes, if it's still all quiet then come up to my room, third on the left."

The girls leaned further forward. Louise was now speaking quietly. "So, what does the prat do? He becomes all messed up and ends up going into my mum's room and gets into bed with her! I reckon you could have heard her screams right across the other side of Preston Park!"

"What was he wearing?" Libby was grinning.

"Thankfully, he had kept his pants on. It's the nearest my mum has come to naked male flesh for years. I doubt she'll ever be the same again," laughed Louise. "He had the bloody cheek to say that he thought something wasn't right when he felt my mum's flannelette nightie! As if..."
"
So, you've split up now?" asked Mandy and Libby in unison.

"No, you're bloody joking. When we did finally get it together, the next night at his place... well... let me just say, ladies... it was a night to remember," Louise fluttered her eyes and performed an exaggerated swoon. All four girls were smiling broadly and even Tracey Albourne managed a slight grin.

"I'll go and top up the jug," announced Libby. "Keep smiling, Trace, he'll be back before you know it."

But it wasn't the return of Nicholas that was troubling her.
It was;
Horrific
Gory
Vile

-0-

On so many occasions, Nicholas had mentioned to her about the weird feeling he had in the pit of his stomach whenever his past was talked about. He had described the experience as if something was alive inside him and when it was disturbed it swirled and rotated uncontrollably as if in torment.

But now Nicholas no longer needed to describe this impression to Tracey Albourne. She was going through it herself. Ever since she had Googled 'Gary Wiseman and Elaine Morse' and viewed Google's response, the feeling emerged churning and seething remorsefully, right inside her. Although Louise Charlton's comical story had given her some respite, it was now back and Tracey Albourne was feeling it bad.

She had to talk.

To her mother? *No*, thought Tracey Albourne, *definitely not*. Although they remained close and her mother adored Nicholas, this subject would be much too much for her.

To his cousin Nancy? No, never. Although they had reached some sort of uneasy truce after their vicious clash ages ago, the relationship was still far too fragile.

To Mr. Braithwaite? Possibly. But she still felt a little guilty the way she had acted up in his classes. Although this was many terms past, she could remember using every opportunity to embarrass him in front of her schoolmates. She thought that maybe he wouldn't believe her anyway.

To Mrs. Baines? She had met Mrs. Baines on a number of occasions when she had accompanied Nicholas to university. They hadn't engaged in much conversation, but she could see the trust between Mrs. Baines and Nicholas was real. So, Tracey Albourne looked up the telephone number of Newham University and asked the receptionist to put her through to Mrs. Baines, telling her, "It's about Nicholas Davison."

-0-

Mrs. Baines welcomed her into the office. A pot of steaming coffee, surrounded by an array of biscuits, lay on the small table where they sat opposite each other.

As they sipped the coffee, Tracey recounted her find at the crematorium and the results of her investigations.
Mrs. Baines sat silently, intently listening, impassively staring straight into Tracey Albourne's hazel eyes.

As Tracey Albourne completed her story, she felt a huge physical relief lift from her shoulders and whirl around her head before drifting silently out of the opened window. She dabbed her eyes with a thoughtfully provided tissue.

As she spoke, Tracey Albourne was surprised to see that Mrs. Baines's face had remained expressionless with just slightly raised eyebrows.

"So, you already knew?"

Mrs. Baines nodded in confirmation. Mrs. Baines held Tracey's hands, gently rubbing the tips of her fingers across Tracey Albourne's carefully manicured nails.

"Yes," she replied, "his cousin Nancy explained everything to me a while back now. It's a shocking story. I was quite taken aback. This must have been tough for you to find out this way?"

Mrs. Baines withdrew her hands and continued talking. "I should explain, Tracey. Your Nicholas has a huge talent. The coaches in Spain this week are going to be in for a shock. I wouldn't be surprised if he returns as their number one, especially in freestyle. You see we've been playing his talent down, not to dampen it, but to keep him away from the spotlight. I've got a pretty good PR team here. I told them that he needs protection, so that he can concentrate solely on his swimming and not to get distracted. They've done a great job... so far," added Mrs. Baines slightly wistfully.

"But what if this gets out?" Tracey Albourne's voice lifted to shrill. "I mean, it could destroy him and his career."

"Now, I think you are getting a little ahead of yourself, Tracey. I'm confident that we can manage this. I hope she won't mind me telling you this but both his, er, cousin Nancy and I will begin to start preparing a way to broach the subject with Nicholas soon after his eighteenth birthday."

"That's coming up soon."

"I know," replied Mrs. Baines.

-0-

Nicholas tactfully waited until his teammates had drifted away before he dropped his canvas holdall and threw his arms around the waiting Tracey Albourne. They clung together in silence for several minutes.

They finally pulled apart. "Much happened whilst I've been away?" asked Nicholas cheerily.

Tracey Albourne stared at the ground.

"Nah... Not much. Come on, I've borrowed a couple of your cousin Nancy's Red Stripes, let's celebrate your return. I've got a great story to tell you about Louise Charlton and her new boyfriend ... this'll kill you."

The couple linked hands and strolled into Preston Park.

Chapter 13. Nicholas and all you can eat

SPORTS NEWS: Local Youngster Takes Three Golds at the National Swimming Championships

'A student at Newham University has stormed to victory in the UK National Swimming Championships. Nicholas Davison (18) prevailed in both the 800 and 1500 metres individual freestyle disciplines and then grabbed a hat trick of gold in the men's 200 metres team relay. Nicholas, who had previously only contended in regional competitions, unexpectedly smashed the UK record in the 800 metres, finishing several lengths ahead of the other competitors. Just a few hours later, he eased to victory in the 1500 metres and his triumphant final leg in the relay guaranteed his third gold and a first for his teammates.

Nicholas lives locally and is currently being coached by the renowned and experienced swimming instructor Mrs. Maureen Baines, who is also a Vice Principal at the College. Commenting on Nicholas's achievements she said, "Nicholas has been training with us for the past two years. His natural ability came to the forefront when he was a pupil at Preston Park Comprehensive and his PE teacher recommended him to us. Nicholas is an extremely talented, albeit reserved young man who wants to concentrate on his swimming and studies," added Mrs. Baines.

We did ask the College for an interview with Nicholas but this was declined. However, they did issue a statement: 'Newham University understands the local and national interest in Nicholas Davison. At this moment in time, he is studying hard for his A Levels and is training daily at the university. Presently, he will not be made available for any interviews as his teachers and coaches are keen for him to continue to pursue both his academic and sporting activities. Any questions relating to Nicholas should be put to Alan Atkinson, who heads the university's public relations department.'

This paper will be closely monitoring Nicholas's progress in the future and will bring news of any further achievements as we learn of them.'

Mary Murray – Sports Editor.

-0-

Tracey Albourne finished reading the report and placed the newspaper back into the rack.

"So now we are going to have to smuggle you in and out of the back entrance with a blanket over your head, just in case the paparazzi are poised with their cameras?" Tracey Albourne saw the alarm in Nicholas's face as she spoke. She smoothed his arm. "I'm joking, Nicholas, don't take it literally, there's not going to be any hacks hanging around the Uni, waiting to pounce. Your anonymity is safe with me around."

Nicholas looked relieved. Nicholas liked being relieved. Nicholas liked having Tracey Albourne guarding his anonymity. Nicholas liked anonymity.

But things had changed.

Nicholas noticed a difference in Tracey Albourne soon after he returned from the Spanish swimming training camp.

She wasn't physically any different. She still had the same hazel eyes; long brown hair and she still wore her tight denim jeans. But her buoyant, bouncy nature, had been replaced by a slightly introspective bearing, punctuated by prolonged periods of silence.

Much to his consternation, he had caught her looking at him with eyes that he suspected portrayed just a hint of sorrowfulness.

This worried Nicholas. He liked her talking. He liked her talking a lot. He liked her looking at him with cheerful eyes.
When they were out together, he felt that she was almost guarding him. Yes, there was this nonsense about a sports editor wanting to track him down for an interview; however, times had moved on. The town's football club was just about to host a top League One team in the televised first round of the FA Cup and the build up to the big game was dominating the local sporting news. Nicholas's exploits in the national swimming championships were now firmly down the list of topical sporting interests.

Alarmingly, Tracey Albourne's actions had actually started to remind him of his previous guardian, Robin. Although Robin was long gone and had been totally different in nature to Tracey Albourne, Robin had been his champion defender in his early years at school.

He shuddered when he remembered those days.

He resolved to find out what event or events had happened that had changed Tracey Albourne's personality so dramatically. Nicholas always struggled to articulate his inner most thoughts, particularly when it came to 'feelings'. But a grim desperation set in - he needed to know. Even with his daily rehearsals, which were practised in the solitary confinement of his bedroom, along with a full-colour picture of Aphrodite standing in for the real Tracey Albourne, it still took him exactly seven days, three hours and forty-two minutes to raise the courage to ask her four simple words. "What's up with you?"

Her response was a lingering and very wet kiss on his lips and a friendly squeeze of his bum. This was followed by, "I love you more than ever... It's just that with my play coming up soon... I've things to think about... you know, remembering my lines and that..." Nicholas knew she wasn't being wholly truthful. But he was happy to accept her explanation.
She said she would 'make it up to him'.

-0-

"Shit... It's her, Mum's back, that's her car... quick, put your clothes on. She'll go mental if she catches us up here." Tracey Albourne leapt out of bed pushing Nicholas away at the same time.

"Don't put the bloody light on, she'll see it from down there."

Tracey Albourne's voice was now a whispered shrill. "Get your stuff together and zip out of the back door." Tracey pulled back the curtain, opening a slim crack. "Good, she's talking to Mrs. Patel; this is your chance, go, quick."

Nicholas whispered back, "For God's sake, Tracey, she must know we're sleeping together, what's the panic?"

Tracey fired back, "Yes she does, probably, but you don't know my mother, she's… well… like… oh I don't know… she doesn't like stuff going on under her nose. Anyway, shut up and stop arguing and grab your things and sod off. I'll call you later."
Tracey Albourne blew Nicholas a kiss.

Nicholas pulled on his sweat shirt and stuffed his remaining belongings into his pockets.

He turned and smiled at Tracey Albourne. "See ya, babe."
Tracey grinned and ushered him away with a flick of her hand.

Nicholas waited, crouched at the side of Tracey Albourne's house. He heard the key turn in the front door and then close. He straightened up and walked quickly towards his own house. He was smiling broadly and there was a definite spring in his step.
He was about halfway down the road when he passed Mr. Thompson, an elderly neighbour who was out walking his dog, Rupert. Nicholas always thought that Rupert was a stupid name to give a dog.
Mr. Thompson gave Nicholas a friendly wave. "Evening, young man, you look very pleased with yourself. Won the lottery?"

Nicholas waved back. "Not quite, Mr. Thompson, but all good here thanks. All OK with you?"

Mr. Thompson nodded. "Apart from being old, but there's nothing I can do about that. See you later." With a tug on Rupert's lead, Mr. Thompson headed towards Preston Park.

Nicholas carried on his way. Mr. Thompson's answer puzzled Nicholas. He thought to himself, *of course you can't help getting old, isn't that what happens to everyone?*

Nicholas arrived at his house. He rummaged through his left trouser pocket and pulled out his keys. He entered through the front door and called out a friendly greeting to his cousin Nancy. The dark shape of his cousin Nancy's head appeared from around the kitchen door.

"Oh, you're back early, what's up?"

Before Nicholas could respond, his cousin Nancy spoke again. "And what's that sticking out of your pocket, the left one?" She stuck out her forefinger in the direction of his trouser pocket. Nicholas looked down and saw a fragment of pink cloth sticking out. He pulled at the cloth and suddenly a pair of pink ladies' mini briefs was in his hand. Confused, he held up the clothing and they both momentarily saw that the briefs had the words 'All You Can Eat' written on the front.

Nicholas quickly stuffed them back into his pocket. His face was rapidly turning a dark crimson. He muttered something like, "I don't know how…"

He didn't finish the sentence.
His cousin Nancy's mouth was terse, but he could see that her eyes positively twinkled.

"Well, Nicholas, either those belong to Tracey Albourne or you're considering transitioning." Nicholas could see she was trying not to laugh.

Nicholas quickly assured her that he was completely content with being a male and that he would return the offending garment back to Tracey Albourne tomorrow.
As he ran upstairs to his bedroom, he heard an enormous guffaw from the kitchen. He was certain that the house actually shook.
He messaged Tracey Albourne. 'I've got something of yours [winking eye, tongue out emoji]'.

Several minutes passed before she replied.

'Thank God for that. I've been looking 4 them everywhere [red face emoji]'.

Smiling, Nicholas opened his back pack and tucked the pink briefs discreetly inside his favourite blue swimming cap. He picked up his book, The Odyssey of Homer.

"All you can eat indeed!"

-0-

Mrs. Baines unceremoniously ushered Nicholas out of her office following their weekly debrief meeting. "I'm expecting a call, Nicholas, an urgent one," explained Mrs. Baines. Nicholas needed very little ushering; he was keen to get home for his tea. He gave her a studious wave and went on his way.

As he left the office, he saw her phone light up. Mrs. Baines picked it up.
"She knows."

Mrs. Baines was speaking. There was a long pause. Finally, she got a response. "How did SHE find out?"

Mrs. Baines replied, "Well, Nancy, despite the way she acts sometimes, she's not stupid is our Miss Albourne. She worked it out for herself. I'm afraid you've got to add her in."

There was another long pause. "OK," came the curt reply and the line fell silent.

-0-

Nicholas tore down the note that had been stuck to his locker door. The handwriting was very familiar, it was from Mrs. Baines. The message was summoning him to call into her office at three o'clock for an 'important meeting about his future'.

Nicholas frowned. As far as he was concerned his future was very much planned out. He would pass all his A Levels; he would then formally enrol at Newham University to study Mathematics and Classics. Of course, he would carry on with his swimming and try to make the next Olympics. Tracey Albourne would remain his partner and when they both had an income, they would eventually marry – the final phase.

Nicholas had it all mapped out. He couldn't imagine any circumstances that would alter this train of events, or phases, as

Nicholas preferred to title the chapters in his life.

As he idly fingered the message between his fingers and thumbs,

Nicholas mused about the phases in his short life:

Phase One: Not much. Swimming. A mum and dad. A strange end.
Phase Two: Living with his grandparents. Grandparents die.
Phase Three: Living with his cousin Nancy. Tracey Albourne becomes his friend.
Phase Four: Still living with his cousin Nancy. Tracey Albourne becomes his lover.

Was he now in Phase Five? Nicholas wasn't sure. Yes, his relationship with Tracey Albourne had 'deepened' and his swimming exploits were now 'turning heads' within the sport. But he was still living in the same house with his cousin Nancy. Nicholas decided that he would officially unveil Phase Five when it was confirmed that his application to enrol at Newham University was successful. He intended take up Uni accommodation.

He gathered up his thoughts, snapped shut the locker door and walked down the corridor to Mrs. Baines's office.

Mrs. Baines called him in.

Nicholas was surprised to see that she wasn't alone. Mrs. Baines was sitting on the edge of her large oak desk. Her hands were placed flat down on either side of her. She was rhythmically swinging her crossed legs. Behind Mrs. Baines, Nicholas spied his cousin Nancy. He saw her staring intently down at her shoes, her large fingers twisting the folds of her plain grey skirt. She didn't acknowledge his arrival. Nicholas looked to his left. Cousin Billy was leaning against a large wooden filing cabinet. His face was filled with his usual expression, a dark scowl. He made no effort to make eye contact with Nicholas.

Nicholas heard a familiar voice coming from the far corner behind him. The voice was low, but he instantly recognised it. "Hi, Nicholas, you, OK?" Tracey Albourne was sitting on a green university chair. She had pulled her legs up to her chest and wrapped her arms around her knees. Nicholas knew what that meant. Tracey Albourne was nervous.

Now Nicholas was nervous. An edgy atmosphere filled the room. Nicholas could almost smell it. Mrs. Baines indicated that he should sit down.

Nicholas sat.

He felt the now very familiar swirl twist remorsefully in the pit of his stomach.

Mrs. Baines spoke softly, "It's about your early life, Nicholas." "Phase One," interjected Tracey Albourne. Nicholas turned and nodded in her direction.

Mrs. Baines ignored her remark. "Do you want to start?" Mrs. Baines looked directly at his cousin Nancy.

His cousin Nancy glanced up. She faced Nicholas and then quickly looked straight past him. Nicholas could see tiny droplets of water appear on her forehead.

She cleared her throat. Nicholas winced.

"This isn't easy for us, Nicholas, but you should know the truth." Taking a deep breath, she blurted out in an unnatural high-pitched squeak, "I'm NOT your cousin," Nancy composed herself, her voice returned almost back to its normal diction, "... and Billy here isn't either." Both Nicholas and Nancy simultaneously turned to look at the still scowling Billy. He nodded.
Nancy continued. Nicholas saw her swallow hard; she was now tugging severely at her skirt.

"And," Nancy stopped and looked at the ceiling. "Your real name isn't Nicholas Davison."

Nicholas heard a little sob from behind him.

Phase Five, he thought.

Chapter 14. Nicholas and what's in a name?

In the space of half an hour, Nicholas had lost two cousins, gained an aunt and uncle and had his name changed.

So, Phase Five was truly open and ready for business.

He knew it was regression, but Nicholas felt compelled to go back to a place where he felt safe. It was early in the morning when he slipped out of the front door and walked briskly to the far side of Preston Park. There stood his favourite old oak tree. Its branches were waving gently in the wind as if they were inviting him in. Soon, he was covered by the swaying bark and an immediate sense of relief sank through him. Nicholas stilled and then slowly slid his body down the broad trunk and drew his knees up to his chin. Unsure about what to do next, Nicholas pushed his hand into his left trouser pocket and pulled out his phone. He began idly flicking through the many apps he had downloaded. Finally, he settled on the video streaming app, Tik Tok. Although his mood was far from euphoric, he did manage the occasional small smile when he viewed a cat attacking a dog or a semi-twinkle when a group of short-skirted girls did a supposedly 'spontaneous' OH NA NA NA Dance.

But Nicholas had little else to smile about.
Following yesterday's revelations about having his real name thrust onto him by his ex-cousins and now aunt and uncle, Nancy and Billy, Nicholas's brain had become blurred. Although the Tik Tok videos were sharp and clear he felt as if he was looking at the rest of the world through frosted glass.

Nicholas soon became bored of dancing girls and aggressive felines, so he closed Tik Tok and opened the camera app. He tapped the 'selfie' icon on the top left of the screen.

Nicholas stared into the face on his phone. The person looking back at him was clearly recognisable. He immediately listed these characteristics:

1. The untidy dark brown hair was definitely Nicholas *Davison's* hair.
2. The pink smooth forehead was emphatically Nicholas *Davison's* forehead.
3. The slightly thin and rather straggly eyebrows certainly belonged to Nicholas *Davison.*

4. The two bright blue unblinking eyes that gazed back at him were unquestionably Nicholas *Davison's* eyes.
5. The slightly long pointed nose, the thin-lipped mouth and the unshaven, stubbly chin, all were undoubtedly Nicholas *Davison's*.

Nicholas lowered his gaze. A Zeus silver chain hung around his neck. He fingered it gently. It was an 18th birthday present from Tracey Albourne to Nicholas Davison. Nicholas momentarily wondered if he would be allowed to keep it, after all, he was now no longer Nicholas Davison.

Feeling a little emotional, Nicholas closed the camera app. The phone's home screen displayed sixteen missed calls, ten voicemails and twelve WhatsApp messages. All of them were from Tracey Albourne except one which was from Nancy. Nicholas ignored them. The calls and messages were for Nicholas Davison and he wasn't Nicholas Davison.

Was Nicholas Davison weird? Nicholas was beginning to think that he was.

-0-

Still trying to clear the fog that was encapsulating his thoughts, Nicholas began walking slowly back across Preston Park. In an attempt to crystallise his feelings, he decided that he would go home, collect his swimming gear and head up to the Neptune Baths for a few lengths. At least when he was in the pool all this business about his name and family would dissolve and dissipate into the clear, chlorinated water. Besides, he needed to step up his training, as Mrs. Baines had told him that a representative from Sport England was due in a few days to assess him.

As he headed up the road a car suddenly screeched up alongside him, its horn was being repeatedly sounded. A startled Nicholas instantly recognised Tracey Albourne's mother's car. It stopped suddenly beside him. The driver's door flung open and he was confronted by a red-eyed and obviously hostile Tracey Albourne.

"Where the fuckin' 'ell have you been?" Tracey Albourne stood directly in front of Nicholas her eyes flashing furiously. Nicholas saw that her hands were clenched into fists. Her face was stony in anger. "I've been calling you, leaving messages, a million times since yesterday and you haven't got back to me. What the fuck is going on?"

Tracey Albourne bit her bottom lip. Tears slid down her now reddening cheeks. She aggressively wiped them away with the back of her still clenched hands.

"Nancy said that you spent all yesterday evening in the pool and then you disappeared early this morning. I was worried sick. We both were." Nicholas could see that she was calming down a little. Her hands were slowly unclenching and her cheeks softening.

"Look, I know all this stuff, is, well you know, like hard to take in, but pushing me away isn't going make it go away. Right?"

Nicholas looked over Tracey Albourne's head and took a deep breath. "Look, I just don't want to be Nicholas Gary Wiseman, right. Because that, like, spells NGW. You know what that means? No? Well, I'll tell you. It means I am a shit wrestler. NGW is New Generation Wrestling. I don't want to be known as a shit wrestler. OK?"

Nicholas exhaled loudly. "And you haven't called me a *million* times. It's more like twenty."

Tracey Albourne almost fell to the floor. She grabbed the wing of the car and steadied herself. More tears fell from her eyes. But this time Nicholas could see that these were tears of laughter. She turned and leant back onto the car. Wearing a broad smile, Tracey Albourne took hold of Nicholas's hand and gently squeezed it. "Nicholas *Davison* you really *are* weird. A shit wrestler? What the... God, you really do crack me up."

"Look, Nicholas, you don't *have* to call yourself Wiseman, you can still be Davison and it's probably best if you do..." Tracey Albourne hesitated. Nicholas looked puzzled. She took a sip of beer from the pint glass in front of her and quickly carried on talking. "I mean that you're known to everyone as Nicholas Davison, so you don't need to change anything. Just carry on as normal." She took a much deeper sip. Nicholas noticed that she avoided making eye contact with his rather perplexed stare.

Normal? thought Nicholas. He wasn't sure what was 'normal' now. In fact, had he ever felt anything was 'normal', so far in his life? Nicholas downed his glass of orange juice. Tracey Albourne was about halfway through her beer. "Look, I'm off to Uni, I've got a session with Mrs. Baines and John Lovell from Sport England is coming along later. I might be in for a bursary or scholarship; this could be the making of me... and us. I'll catch you later." Nicholas kissed Tracey Albourne lightly on her cheek. He stood up to go, and then paused in thought. Nicholas asked, "What did you mean about 'probably for the best'?" Nicholas wrinkled his eyebrows.

Tracey Albourne kept her drink near her lips. Head down, she spoke into the glass. "Nothing... really... sweetheart. It's like it's just best if you like, you know... keep being a Davison... I think it suits you," she added rather unconvincingly. "Anyway, you get going, you can't keep our Maureen waiting, now, can you? Think of all the loot that's coming your way!"

"It's not often that I agree with her, but this time Tracey Albourne is right, you don't need to change anything, you should stay as Nicholas Davison, it's the best thing," Nancy hoped that her voice sounded calm and reassuring.

Nicholas nodded.

Nancy tilted her head to one side, "Now is there anything else you want to ask?"

Nicholas hesitated and began idly twiddling with his phone between his fingers and thumb. He looked up at Nancy; he noticed that a glint of perspiration had formed just above her upper lip. Speaking softly, he said, "Why did you and Billy pretend to be my cousins when you are really my aunt and uncle?"

Nancy wiped her mouth with a bright white handkerchief. She paused before replying. "We were trying to protect you... Sorry no... I mean, we thought that if you regarded us as your equals instead of a type of parental figures, that you would, you know, feel more comfortable." Nicholas wasn't convinced that this was the real reason, but in the absence of a better explanation, he accepted it. Nicholas tucked away his phone. He noticed there was a WhatsApp message from Tracey Albourne. He ignored it.

He carried on speaking. "There's one other thing. When I was at my grandmother's funeral, I saw three coffins, two large and one small in between them. Was that my father, mother and, I don't know, a brother or sister, or something?"

Nancy's eyes widened. She began rubbing her hands together as if they had suddenly become frozen. After a short pause she replied, "Nicholas, I don't know what you are on about. At your grandmother's funeral there was just one coffin, and that was hers. You couldn't have seen three, that's impossible."

Nicholas replied, "I did. I know what I saw, three coffins, two large and one small in between them."

Nancy shuffled, agitated, on her chair, the bead of perspiration reappeared on her top lip.

Nicholas carried on talking, "When I was sat next to you, I shut my eyes and opened them, I definitely saw three coffins, and you even told me off for doing it! I'd been to that crematorium before, I was certain of it then and I am still convinced." Nicholas's voice had slid up an octave.

Nancy's now not so bright, white handkerchief made a second appearance. "Look, I'm not buying this, you COULDN'T have seen three coffins, it's impossible, but yes, you had been there before and that time there were three coffins, and again yes, there were two large and one small. You must have got things mixed up... in your head," she added rather unconvincingly.

Nancy hesitated, and her eyes started to glisten. Nicholas felt a large lump form in his throat.

Nancy wiped her eyes, and speaking in almost a whisper, she said, "One of the large coffins belonged to your father who also happened to be my brother, Gary."

"And the other two?" asked Nicholas.

"Gary's partner, her name was Elaine and the small one was her young daughter, Brooke." Nancy was now openly crying. Nicholas spontaneously reached out and held her hands.

They both sat in an embarrassed, uncomfortable silence. Nicholas withdrew his hands. He felt the familiar swirling in his stomach rise and whirl remorsefully through his insides. He believed that he was about to vomit, when two new thoughts suddenly crashed, like a couple of meteorites simultaneously hitting a planet, into his mind.

"So, my mother is still alive?"

"Yes," replied Nancy, wiping away her tears. "She is."
Nicholas nodded.

"And one other question... those three coffins... with three people inside...

Was I, you know, like, in some way involved in their deaths?"

Nicholas saw Nancy nod very slightly.

-0-

Nicholas and Tracey Albourne, in an unrehearsed, spontaneous unison, pushed open the heavy wooden doors of the Preston Arms.

The bar was practically deserted.

"So, the drinks are on you then, Nicholas Davison or should I say, the next *Michael Phelps*?" Nicholas smiled. He ordered two pints. Tracey Albourne hugged him so tightly that he almost knocked them over. "You've got the sponsorship then?"

Nicholas nodded and took a deep swig. "It's called a sports scholarship," corrected Nicholas, "basically I get paid for swimming as long as I'm at Uni."

He noticed that she suddenly looked dejected. Her face had fallen and her eyes were sad.

"What's up, Trace? Aren't you pleased for me?"

Tracey Albourne grabbed Nicholas's arm, tears formed in her eyes and then one slowly dropped down her cheek. She gulped, "This isn't going to make a difference to *US*, is it? I mean you'll be famous and I'm just, like a, you know, a person."

Nicholas pulled her close. "Shut up," he commanded, trying hard to sound masterful. "Of course, it makes no difference, whatever happens, I'll still be Nicholas Davison, now that you and Nancy have told me I've got to be, and you'll still be the ONE and ONLY Tracey Albourne, my partner and soulmate. So, stop snivelling and get the beers in, we are celebrating tonight!"

"Oh, and yes, I've got something else to tell you, but that can wait." Tracey Albourne fired him a puzzled look. "Good or bad?" she asked.

Nicholas hesitated, "Umm... Well, like, I'm sure a bit could be quite good... But another bit could be very bad... I'm not entirely sure, I'll tell all later." He playfully shoved a slightly perplexed Tracey Albourne in the direction of the bay window.

Chapter 15. Nicholas and Desdemona

Nicholas's hopes of a clandestine entry into the theatre lobby were instantly thwarted. He had only been in the crowded room for a few seconds when he heard his name being called. "Nicholas, NICHOLAS, over here, yoo hoo, over here, it's us, hi ya." Nicholas glanced over to the 'yoo hoos'. He immediately spotted two of his ex-classmates, Louise Charlton and Mandy Johnson. They were both waving at him furiously. The two young women scurried over towards him, gently nudging away anyone that had the audacity to get in their way.

They both stood either side of him like sentries on guard and grabbed his arms. They were dressed similarly in rather elegant long dresses that sparkled under the ceiling lights. Nicholas looked at them from foot to head; he imagined that their dresses could light into tiny little sparks ready to ignite. Louise had her blonde hair arranged in a tight bun, whereas Mandy's long dark hair flowed down her exposed white shoulders.

Christ, how everyone has changed since we left school, thought Nicholas. He momentarily wondered if he looked much different. Not a lot was his instant conclusion, particularly as he had been immediately identified by Louise and Mandy the very instant, he walked through the doorway.

Mandy shoved a glass of sparkling wine in his hand. Louise spoke first, "We knew you'd be here, our Trace's debut. We knew you wouldn't miss it."

Mandy sipped from her glass leaving a deep red lipstick stain on the rim and looked Nicholas up and down. "You could have dressed up a bit though, the opening night is usually a black-tie affair and let's face it you're the co-star's partner," she said slightly reprovingly. Nicholas thought that he had 'dressed up'. He was wearing his favourite Gant black jeans and a neatly ironed white, open-necked, Ralph Lauren shirt. He shrugged his shoulders, "I'm going incognito, I don't want to put her off," he said rather unconvincingly. Mandy and Louise each smiled a 'tut tut'.

Suddenly, Louise thrust her third finger of her left hand under Nicholas's nose and provocatively wheeled it around. "See," she said excitedly. Out of the corner of his eye Nicholas spotted Mandy's face droop slightly.

Nicholas examined the diamond and silver engagement ring. "Felix? When's the big day?"

Louise dropped her hands to her side. "Oh, we haven't finalised that yet, he's going for a promotion and when he gets that then we can set a date, it'll be a couple of years, perhaps."

Nicholas nodded, smiled and turned to Mandy. "Are you still at home, Mandy?" he enquired. He noticed her eyes glistened slightly.

"Yes," she replied softly. "It's me mam; she's not getting any better. I have to keep an eye on her, you know, like, how it is." Nicholas gently squeezed her arm. Tracey Albourne had told him about Mandy's mother's early onset dementia, and he knew she was doing a hell of a lot more than just 'keeping an eye on her'. Mandy brightened up, "Anyway, we're here tonight and your girl's gonna kill us, so come on, Nick, you're going to be me and this 'ere engaged person's escort for the evening, let's grab some seats." Nicholas was duly whisked away with Louise and Mandy on each arm.

Nicholas was faintly aware of the story of Othello. He tried his hardest to follow the performance but, each time Tracey Albourne, aka Desdemona, was on the stage, his eyes were totally transfixed on her. During the 'death' scene near the end, he had to muster himself from leaping from his seat and climbing onto the stage to bash Othello (played by another ex-classmate – Kofi Ajanlekoko) on the head, with a 'leave her alone!'

At the end, both Louise and Mandy had watery eyes as the cast took their respective bows. Desdemona was presented with a large bouquet of flowers and Nicholas was sure she got the biggest cheer from the very appreciative audience.

With the house lights filling the auditorium, the trio got up and, in silence, headed towards the lobby. Louise spoke first. "Phew, that was some performance; I'd forgotten what a great tragedy Othello was. I don't think I could ever hear 'Prick Willow' again without bursting into tears! And that Iago, what a complete bastard, he was."

"Tracey was bloody brilliant, you didn't tell us that she could act like that," admonished Mandy, looking directly at Nicholas. "You must be very proud of her... Oh, hang on, here's our taxi. Right, Nick, thanks for a great evening." Mandy and Louise reached up and kissed either side of his face; then they dived into the back seat of the cab. They both gave him a friendly wave as the taxi made its way out of the car park.

Nicholas suddenly felt light-headed. He quickly sat on a nearby bench watching the stream of cars filter away. His mind was racing. *What did Louise say? Iago was a complete bastard? He wasn't half as much a bastard as this totally complete bastard, sitting here. All this time, here I was wrapped up in my own tawdry world of non-cousins, changing names, visions of coffins, Greek gods, swimming and everything else, I'd hadn't realised what a talent had been by my side all this time. I should be ashamed of myself. I AM ashamed of myself.*

Nicholas's thoughts were abruptly interrupted. He felt a light nudge in his side. "Well. How did I do?" Tracey Albourne's soft voice whispered in his left ear. Nicholas looked across at her. Her deep hazel eyes gazed enquiringly into his.

He paused.

"You were... Oh what the hell, you were... Fucking brilliant!"

Tracey Albourne looked stunned. "I thought that you didn't approve of swearing?"

Nicholas grabbed her around the waist and picked her up and swung her around. "Well, I do tonight, 'cos you were, 'kin brilliant," he replied.

Grinning broadly, he whispered in her ear, "Fancy a bit of 'tupping' later on? I think Nancy's out all night." His tongue just touched the tip of her ear lobe.

Tracey Albourne winced. "Do you know what tupping is?"

Nicholas shrugged. "Sex?"

Tracey Albourne laughed. "Yes, with sheep." Nicholas reddened and clenched his teeth.

Tracey looked impishly up at him and winked. "Baaa!" she said.

"I'll call for a cab. By the way, kissing Kofi is a bit like kissing a horse, all hot breath, lips and teeth. Yuk! Though now I come to think of it, it's actually no different from when we were both at school."

Nicholas pretended not to hear that last sentence.

-0-

"Now are you absolutely sure that you don't want me with you?" Nicholas and Tracey Albourne were sitting in her mother Sharon's car in the car park of 'Madeley and Johnson, Solicitors and Attorneys at Law'.

Nicholas leaned across the passenger seat and held Tracey Albourne's hand. "Nah, I'm cool with this, he just wants to talk to me about some financial stuff, I reckon it's to do with this scholarship I've just got, and it's no big deal. Anyway, it'll make a nice change; me actually speaking to him, every time I've met him before he couldn't wait to get away from me, it's like I was a leper or something!"

"Anyway, haven't you got a meeting at the theatre?" Tracey Albourne nodded. She loosened Nicholas's grip on her hand and placed it on her knee, "Yeah, some sort of debrief, our two weeks ended last night, the director wants to talk to all the cast about it."

Nicholas squeezed her knee, "It went down well, didn't it?" Tracey nodded again, she looked slightly crestfallen. "Yep... Look... Anyway, if you're sure you're OK I'll get off," she pushed his hand away and started the engine.

Nicholas jumped out of the car, "Call ya later, babe, have fun!"

-0-

Nicholas stood at the oak panelled door bearing the transcription *'Welcome to Madeley and Johnson – please press the bottom button to call reception.'* Nicholas smoothed down his jeans with the palms of his hands and then duly pressed the intercom, "Hi, it's Nicholas Davison here, I've come to see Mr. Madeley." Nicholas heard a short acknowledgement and the door buzzed open. Nicholas stepped inside.

"Ah, Nicholas, you look well, do come in and sit down, Mrs.

Atkinson has made us some tea and biscuits, please help yourself." Mr. Madeley rose to shake Nicholas's hand. Nicholas peered around the room. It was oak panelled from ceiling to floor, with a large wooden desk in the far corner. The top of the desk was strewn with papers and a rather old-fashioned inkwell with three black pens sat in a brass holder right in the centre. Each wall was adorned with an array of slightly faded framed certificates and awards, each bearing the name of 'Ralph J. Madeley'.

Mr. Madeley indicated that Nicholas should sit. He placed a cup of tea and saucer into his hand, and Nicholas noticed that a digestive biscuit was lodged rather precariously on the edge of the saucer. He grabbed it before it fell.

Mr. Madeley sat down opposite Nicholas; he was clutching a large manilla coloured, albeit slightly battered, file in his hands. Nicholas spotted that it was titled – 'The Wiseman Family'.

"Right, Nicholas, let's get down to things. I gather congratulations are in order, well done for achieving this scholarship, a bright future for you is unfolding." Mr. Madeley paused and leant down and opened his familiar black briefcase, it was the very same briefcase that Nicholas had spied so many times before. Mr. Madeley pulled out some papers and slipped them inside the manilla folder; he then opened the folder onto his lap and put on some rather large black framed spectacles.

"I know your Aunt Nancy hasn't mentioned this to you, but she and I are joint trustees of a trust fund held in your name." Mr. Madeley paused again and sipped some tea. "A reasonably large sum of money has accrued over the years and under the terms of the trust this passes over to you, now you have reached the age of eighteen." Mr. Madeley paused again and took another sip.

"However, I have taken the liberty of seeking some advice from a financial expert and she suggested that we review the redemption of the trust, in view of your recent award from Sport England."

Mr. Madeley could see that Nicholas looked slightly distracted, "That's why I asked you here today, Nicholas, to discuss this." Mr. Madeley stared directly at Nicholas with his hands folded over the opened manilla folder.

Nicholas looked at Mr. Madeley and then looked down at the manilla folder sitting in his lap. "Can I ask you a question, Mr. Madeley?"

Mr. Madeley nodded his assent, "Of course, dear boy, fire away."

Nicholas took a sharp intake of breath, then calmly he said, "Are you OUR solicitor, you know for the whole family, you know like a *Wiseman Family Solicitor*?"

Mr. Madeley, taken aback, frowned. "Yes, I suppose I am; why do you ask?"

Nicholas examined the back of his hands. "Well, my real name was, or still is, Wiseman, correct?" Mr. Madeley continued to look puzzled, his head tilted slightly to the left. He nodded slowly.
"So," Nicholas continued, speaking slowly, "you're *my* solicitor as well then?"
Mr. Madeley closed the cover of the manilla folder. "Yes, I suppose I am, but where is this leading to, Nicholas, we really must get to the point of this meeting, namely your trust fund."
Nicholas sat on the edge of his seat. Speaking almost inaudibly, Nicholas whispered, "Was I in some way involved in the deaths of my father and the two Morse people, Elaine and her daughter, Brooke?"

Mr. Madeley let out an enormous gasp; Nicholas felt his breath blow into his face. "Now, now, Nicholas, oh dear, now, now, sorry, but this isn't in my brief, you will have to talk to your aunt and uncle about this." Mr. Madeley stood up and walked over to his desk, held onto the side for support and wiped his forehead with a large blue handkerchief.

Nicholas tried to remain calm, although the now far too familiar swirling in his insides began starting to take control, rising and falling mercilessly in unison with his breathing. Nicholas pleaded, "Please just tell me… one way or the other… PLEASE TELL ME. Mr. Madeley this is *killing me.* I have to … I NEED to know."

Mr. Madeley stood still. He removed his spectacles and wiped them on the blue handkerchief. He looked down at Nicholas.
"Oh well," he sighed, "I'll probably get dismissed for telling you this, but as I am your solicitor and you are my client, I will give you, my answer."

The air in the room stood still. Nicholas felt a bead of perspiration slide down his back, and the swirling feeling in his stomach suddenly stood still, paused in anticipation.

"Yes, Nicholas you were involved but, Nicholas you weren't responsible for their deaths... But ... you were there, you witnessed it all... the whole horrific, gory, vile mess."

Nicholas immediately felt the swirling in his insides dissipate. Gone, dissolved; vanished in an instant... Just a vague hollow emptiness was left in their wake. It was as if a physical part of him had been removed... Somehow, he knew this was forever.

A sense of relief fell over Nicholas. He gripped the sides of his armchair and stood up. Speaking brightly, Nicholas tapped Mr. Madeley lightly on the arm, "Thanks, Mr. Madeley, I need some air, can we discuss this trust business another day?"

Mr. Madeley wiped his eyes on the back of his hands, "Of course, dear boy." As Nicholas turned to go, he laid a light hand on Nicholas's shoulder, "You should talk to Miss Wiseman about this, Nancy, get an appointment with Dr. Jonathan Hazel, he is the best person, he'll make it all clear, speak to your aunt. Please."

Nicholas headed towards the door. He turned and saw Mr. Madeley holding onto his desk and chair staring hard into the carpet. "Sorry I had to ask, Mr. Madeley, but when no one will tell you anything, I had to ask, sorry."

Mr. Madeley didn't look up.

Nicholas walked into the sunlight.

He knew now that Phase One was opening up; it was only a matter of time. All he had to do was to get that username and password to open up the firewall that was blocking his mind. He didn't know exactly why, but suddenly he now felt these were almost within his grasp. "Dr. J. Hazel, you're next," he said to himself.

As Nicholas strode towards the bus stop, he sent a WhatsApp message to Tracey Albourne – 'All, OK? I'm going 2 the pool for a bit, c ya 2nite. Luv ya x'

Chapter 16 4 U Nick

The clock beside his bed glowed 4.34am.

Nicholas was unsettled.

His armpits were uncomfortably damp and there was a curious dry taste in his mouth. He turned onto his back and adjusted his pillows.

Nicholas stared, bleary-eyed, at the thin crack that meandered across the ceiling. Then it hit him.

He had just witnessed The Dream. Two nights in a row he had had the same dream. But this time it was different. This time he could recall the whole sequence from start to finish.

Nicholas pulled his duvet up close and mentally rolled away the boulder that had been blocking his mind.

The Dream... An Out of Body Experience written and narrated by
Nicholas Davison

It started with him sitting alone on the floor of a darkened room. He
was staring at a computer screen. There didn't appear to be a
keyboard or mouse or any other means to operate it. The screen
was blank apart from two boxes with the titles, 'username' and
'password'. Underneath the boxes appeared an 'enter' button. A
username had already been inserted, 'Wiseman1', but the
password was obscured by eight asterisks. A cursor in the shape of
an arrow appeared from the bottom left and slowly started to move
across the screen. The cursor stopped at the 'enter' button and
tapped it. A new page opened displaying two yellow files, named
'Images' and 'Videos'. The cursor hesitated momentarily then slid
towards the 'Images' file and hovered over it.
A message instantly popped up; *The file cannot be opened because
there are problems with the contents'*. The cursor stilled and then
glided across to the 'Videos' file and the same response appeared,
*'The file cannot be opened because there are problems with the
contents'.*

The cursor then began to move frantically back and forth between
the two files until suddenly the sequence started to dissipate and
Nicholas began to rouse.
The End

Still in a semi-unconscious stupor, Nicholas returned the boulder
back into its place and turned over, and he quickly fell back to sleep.
Sleep was crucial tonight. He had an important meeting in the
morning.

-0-

"So, you knew all along and you didn't say anything?" Nicholas was standing in front of Tracey Albourne, his eyes glaring and his hands clenched into fists. Tracey Albourne looked down at her knees and then she drew them up to her chest. There was no eye contact, but the tension generated between the couple was palpable. Even the normally curious ducks that roamed around Preston Park Lake were keeping their distance.

Nicholas waited for her answer.

Tracey Albourne straightened up. "Don't look at me like that... Please." She paused and sucked in a mouthful of air.

"OK, so, what was I supposed to say...? Something like, 'Hi, Nicholas have you had a good swimming session today, oh and by the way, I've just found out that when you were six years old, you, like, witnessed the totally sick murder of your father, his partner and a seven-year-old girl.' It's not the sort of thing that trips easily off the tongue... Is it... well... IS IT?"

There was a moment's silence. She loosened the grip on her knees and beckoned Nicholas to sit beside her. He obeyed.

"Besides they... you know, your cuz... sorry, your Aunt Nancy and Uncle Billy promised me they were going to come completely clean to you soon."

Nicholas held her hand. She felt him relax slightly. "So, when did you find out? How?"

Tracey Albourne gently squeezed Nicholas's arm. "Well, it was when we went the Crem. I spotted the name Gary Wiseman and two others cremated at the same time, so, when I, like, got back indoors, I Googled the names and, well, there were loads of news reports about it."

Nicholas opened his mouth to speak.

Tracey Albourne put her index finger to his lips. "I know what you are going to say. Why didn't I tell you there and then? But I just couldn't, I didn't want to hurt you, or worse, you know, damage you mentally or something. Besides, once I'd talked it over with Nancy, she promised she'd, you know, like, sort it out."

Nicholas stared across the lake. His eyes followed a family of three, a man and woman on the far side, playing catch with a young boy. Nicholas guessed the boy was about six or seven years old. Tracey Albourne nudged him gently, she was now speaking softly. "So, this Doctor Hazel fella told you everything today, did he?" Nicholas nodded and turned to Tracey Albourne. "Yep, everything right from the very beginning, you know, Phase One in its entirety. It was really weird. It was as if he was telling me a story about someone else, you know, far away and not MY early life."

Nicholas hesitated and rubbed his nose.

Tracey Albourne's raised eyebrows were the signal for Nicholas to continue.

Nicholas inhaled. "First off he told me that my dad lectured at Newham University. He left abruptly. It was immediately after he dumped my mother; apparently, he couldn't handle her 'erratic behaviour'. It seems she was a bit 'psycho', so basically, he did a runner with me, and a fellow lecturer, who I guess he was already having a fling with, and her young daughter. He later claimed in his resignation letter that he 'feared for our safety'."

"Well, he got that bit right," whispered Tracey Albourne.

"Anyway," continued Nicholas, "we moved to Warwick. Did you know he was a professor in mathematics? He had resigned before Mrs. Baines joined, so they never met. But now I know why Nancy was so vehemently opposed to me going there. I think she thought someone there might recognise me or something. In fact, quite a few things that have happened recently have started to slot into place."

Nicholas gripped her hand tightly. "But I'm still fazed about not remembering anything about living in Warwick with my father and this Elaine lady and her daughter. She was called Brooke, you know, that's quite an unusual name, isn't it?"

Tracey Albourne rolled her eyes, "Yes, it is a bit unusual. But go on." "Well, after it happened, they brought me back to live here, with my grandparents. I was schooled at home until I was ten, then I was sent off to Preston Park Comp. You know, Trace, I can't recall any of it. I mean, I remember both my grandparents quite clearly, but my life before I'd started at school is now completely blank. I used to sometimes remember bits and pieces, but just recently the whole lot has gone."

"I'm pleased they chose PPC, because that's where I met you," whispered Tracey Albourne, reaching up to give Nicholas a gentle kiss on his left cheek.

"Yes, and at first, you were bloody horrible to me," retorted Nicholas.

Tracey Albourne blushed slightly, "I ALWAYS fancied you... I just had an odd way of showing it." She gave him another kiss. "Anyway, let's not talk about that now. What else did Doctor Hazel tell you?" "Well, he said that it wasn't unusual for the mind to block out traumatic events, especially in children, he reckoned that I am suffering from... now what did he call it... Hmm... ah yes, infantile amnesia... and most likely PTSD."

"I've heard of PTSD, but what the flip is infantile amnesia?" Tracey Albourne looked puzzled.

"Doctor Hazel said something like it's the inability of a person to retrieve episodic memories, whatever that means, and post-traumatic stress disorder is common in soldiers after they had witnessed a traumatic event, you know like the death of a fellow soldier. He said had I been diagnosed and properly counselled when I was young, they could have opened up my memories and got me to come to terms with what I saw. But the family just deleted the whole event and never spoke about it, which must have had some effect on me. He also said that had I been treated, he reckoned that I wouldn't have had such a rough time when I finally went to school. Thinking back, I know I acted weird at times, you know, not making any friends and the like, well, until me and you got together. You must have been mental to take up with me."

Tracey Albourne smiled and nodded.

"Oh, thanks for agreeing with that," smiled Nicholas.
It was the first time he had smiled in days.

-0-

Nicholas was lying on the top of his bed. The bare walls of his university room mustered a gloomy atmosphere, the curtains were drawn and the eerie half-light filled the room.

Nicholas felt troubled.

Nicholas didn't like being troubled.

He hadn't told Tracey Albourne everything about his meeting with Doctor Hazel. There was one piece that he had kept to himself. It was the subject of his mother's paintings.

Doctor Hazel had explained that there hadn't been a trial. Although the triple murder appeared to have been meticulously planned and savagely carried out, it was deemed that she was unfit to plead. A psychiatrist's report had recommended that she should be committed to a secure psychiatric hospital, indefinitely, for treatment. A judge agreed and so, Nicholas's mother, Janet Wiseman, was committed to Rampton under the care of Doctor J. Hazel and his team.

Doctor Hazel went on to tell Nicholas that during their many sessions with him or another doctor, they had asked Janet what she could recall about her family. She would only refer to her brother Billy. She was totally adamant that the only family member she had was Billy. She repeatedly said that she had always been a single woman with no partner or children.

Doctor Hazel said that recreation was part of her therapy and Janet had mentioned that she would like to paint. Nicholas's Uncle Billy, during one of his visits, had taken in all the art materials, so she was set up.

Doctor Hazel had showed Nicholas two of her paintings. Nicholas's face had turned pale when he viewed the pictures.

They both accurately detailed a teenage boy swimming. One was set in the sea, the other in a swimming pool. The boys in the picture had an uncanny and rather disturbing resemblance to Nicholas. Same colour and length of hair, a similar build and they were both wearing a shade of blue trunks almost exactly the same as a pair that Nicholas possessed. In one painting the boy was also wearing a blue swimming cap akin to one Nicholas often wore. Doctor Hazel confirmed that there were "many more like this." One even depicted the same boy standing at the top of a podium with what appeared to be the five Olympic rings in the background.

Doctor Hazel said that he couldn't offer any plausible explanations why she had chosen this particular subject for her work. When Janet was quizzed over the content of her paintings, she had simply replied, "I paint what's in my head."

Even with his eyes tightly shut, Nicholas could clearly see images of the two paintings. A shiver shook the length of his body. Nicholas pulled the duvet up over his shoulders and sat himself upright. He checked his phone for messages. There was just one; a red heart emoji from Tracey Albourne.

-0-

Tracey Albourne was in her bedroom. She was on her laptop, revisiting the news reports of the so-called, 'Wiseman Murders'. The journalists had clearly revelled in writing extremely graphic descriptions of the murder weapon, a large kitchen knife, the scene and its aftermath, but one paragraph surpassed them all. It had jumped out of the screen and imprinted itself indelibly into her brain. With tears in her eyes, she picked up her phone and sent a heart shaped emoji to Nicholas.

'... and the assailant had daubed a wall at the murder scene with the phrase '4 U NICK' written in the blood of one of the poor victims... possibly an obscure and macabre reference to her estranged six-year-old son, Nicholas, who had witnessed the whole gory incident, before being rescued by a neighbour...'

Chapter 17. Nicholas the Golden Boy

Three years later
Nancy and Billy could barely speak to each other as they entered Preston Park.
"I've never seen so many people," mused Nancy.
An earnest looking teenager, wearing a yellow sweat shirt with the word 'STEWARD' printed on the front and back, gently tugged at Nancy's arm and ushered the pair into the temporary grandstand.

"They must have come from all over the county," added a slightly bewildered Billy.

"All over the COUNTRY," interjected the teen steward. "We've even had a contingent up from Kent, they came up in a minibus. He's the poster boy of the games," he added in a wistful whisper. "*Everyone* wants a piece of him.

"Anyway, these are your seats." The teenager flicked his thumb in the direction of a row of seats marked 'VIP GUESTS'. He then marched away to greet the next spectators, three young women. As Nancy settled in her seat, she spotted Mr. Brathwaite, Nicholas's former school teacher, who was sat alone directly in front of the pair. She tapped him lightly on the shoulder and whispered into his ear.

"This is all down to you, you know, Mr. Braithwaite, you're the one that first spotted Nicholas's talents." Nancy pointed at the crowd of people that had gathered in front of the stage.

Looking over Mr. Braithwaite's head, she scanned the setting. She sighed slightly as she spotted a huge picture of Nicholas that was being beamed in full colour as the backdrop to the stage. The image depicted Nicholas smiling cheerfully and clutching six round silver and gold medals to his bare chest.
A man wearing blue jeans and a multi-coloured short sleeved shirt was standing at the side of the picture. He had a microphone to his lips. Nancy vaguely recognised him as the morning shows DJ from the local radio station that she occasionally listened to in the kitchen. Such was the noise emanating from the crowd, she couldn't quite make out what he was saying, but there was plenty of cheering and clapping. Some were even making the horrible 'whooping' noise that Americans were so particularly fond of shouting.

Mr. Braithwaite turned and smiled at Nancy, "Call me John, all the 'Mr. Braithwaite' stuff is for school only and anyway, don't be modest, you played a big part in his development. He wouldn't be here today if it wasn't for you. Well, both of you." Mr. Braithwaite leaned forward and shook Billy's and Nancy's hands in turn. He continued speaking. "Maybe I was the first to take him swimming, but others brought him along, you know, Joe Fahey, Maureen Baines, but you gave him the stability and support in the background. You should be very proud of yourselves."

Nancy blushed and dabbed at her eyes with a pink cotton handkerchief. Billy's normally permanent scowl relented momentarily.

"And don't forget Tracey Albourne."

Nancy, Billy and Mr. Braithwaite all swung towards the voice. A woman, probably in her early twenties, was addressing them. Her face was stony, and her lips were pursed. Her eyes were fastened on the trio.

"She stuck by him through all of this. I mean at school he was a bit of a loner, you know, like a geek, she got right behind him. She sort of, you know, well, like er... well she 'normalised' him... in a way."

Mr. Braithwaite immediately recognised one of his former students, Mandy Johnson.

"He couldn't have done it without *her*." Mandy Johnson turned her back on them in an exaggerated flounce and began speaking to her companions.

All three were momentarily silenced. They looked at each other with raised eyebrows. Mr. Braithwaite muttered something inaudible. Billy and Nancy just glanced at each other unsmiling. They turned back to face the crowd, which was now being hushed by the multi-coloured shirt wearing MC.

There was an almighty roar as Nicholas climbed onto the stage. Nancy frowned as she saw Tracey Albourne holding Nicholas's hand. Her frown softened as she watched Nicholas approach the microphone and Tracey Albourne let go of his hand and stepped back.

There were thanks aplenty. Nancy's pink cotton handkerchief made a brief reappearance when she heard her name mentioned. Mr. Braithwaite, Mr. Fahey and Mrs. Baines all got special acknowledgements, plus a few others that she didn't immediately recall.

Her frown returned sharply when she witnessed Nicholas pulling Tracey Albourne to his side and then he kissed her on the cheek. This brought the crowd to deafening crescendo.
Nancy's frown remained unmoved.

-0-

Nancy and Billy were walking side by side strolling in silence towards Preston Park's tiny car park. Eventually, Nancy remarked to Billy that he seemed deep in thought.

"Penny for them, Billy, what's on your mind?"

Billy stopped and rested his backside on the wing of his car. He rubbed his chin and looked directly at Nancy. Speaking slowly, he said, "You know, do you think all of THIS," Billy waved his arms in the direction of the masses of people now heading away from the park, "would have happened if my sister hadn't done what she did to your brother all those years ago? I mean, if Nicholas had stayed with Gary and Elaine, he wouldn't have had all this, would he?"

Nancy leaned beside Billy. "No, he wouldn't have, no chance. Don't get me wrong, Gary was a good father to Nicholas, but no way would he have encouraged a sporting career. He was firmly an academic, Nicholas would have ended up as a teacher or lecturer or something.

"Now he is a millionaire sporting celebrity, with the world at his feet," she added quietly. "Maybe some good came out of the evil... In the end."

Nancy watched as Billy took a large intake of breath, she could see his hands shaking. He took out a paper tissue and wiped his forehead.

"That's what's bothering me. Look I've never told anyone this, but..." Billy clasped his hands as if he was about to pray.

"Go on," Nancy held Billy's elbow gently. "Go on," she repeated.
"Well, it's like this. When we were young, you know, just kids at home, Janet would often say weird things. It was like she could predict the future. Some things were quite simple, you know like, 'don't go to school down Brompton Avenue as there has been an accident and the road will be blocked' and it was, but the accident had happened a couple of hours AFTER she had said it."

Billy opened the car door and pulled out a bottle of water. He unscrewed the top and took a deep swig.
"There were other things as well. One day at dinner she suddenly stood up all pale and shaking saying that Dad had had an accident at work and was being taken to hospital. Guess what, fifteen minutes later we had a phone call from Dad's place saying he had burnt his hands and they had driven him to the Burns unit at the local hospital. As it turned out he wasn't badly hurt, but how the hell did she know that it was going happen?

"There were others as well, in fact too many to recall. It was like she had some sort of sixth sense. Mum and Dad just dismissed the accident incident as a lucky guess, but I knew differently."

Billy took another sip of water. Nancy held his elbow a little tighter. "And those paintings she does in hospital, they are of Nicholas, I'm one hundred percent certain of it, they are the spitting image of him. Look, one even was of him underneath the Olympic rings. How the bloody hell does she know what he looks like? She's not bloody well clapped eyes on him for years."

Billy paused; he wiped the palms of his hands down his trouser legs. "Remember the scene? She wrote '4 U NICK' on the wall in that poor kid's blood. It meant nothing at the time, you know, it was just dismissed as a mad woman's rambling." Billy hesitated and looked at Nancy with glistening eyes. "But now there is all this..."

"You're NOT saying she knew that without her..." Nancy sought the right words, "intervention ... none of this would have happened, you know, Nicholas's success at the Olympics and everything?

Surely not...?"

Billy nodded. "I am, she knew it, I'm bloody convinced of it."
"She did it for Nicholas."

-0-

<u>One year later</u>

Nicholas seized a rare opportunity to slip away.

Preston Park was quiet.

Autumn was descending and the wildlife that swam and roamed the banks of Preston Park Lake were preparing for the darker, colder evenings. Nicholas leaned against the old oak tree that had served as his silent companion and listener-in-chief so many times in the past. His hands were buried deep into his coat pockets and his thoughts buried deep in contemplation.

The memories of that rather puzzling homecoming parade had progressively slipped unconsciously into the farthest corners of Nicholas's mind. So much more had happened since the day he was fêted as a homecoming hero.

In the cool air, Nicholas sensed now was the right time to unravel the events.

He used his time-honoured process - a list:
1. The car accident and the injury to his arm that eventually called a halt to his swimming career
2. The offer of a three-year contract from Eurosport to become a co-presenter and commentator on all televised swimming events around the world
3. Then the offer from the BBC to host a new sporting challenge gameshow alongside a Swedish film star
4. The departure of Tracey Albourne to Los Angeles, United States

As in many times past Nicholas delved into each subject in random order.

Tracey Albourne had been noticed. In a whirlwind few months, she went from dedicated amateur actor, to aspiring professional, and with the help of her newly acquired agent, a part, albeit a small one, in a Hollywood movie. They talked about it; she said she couldn't turn it down, he remembered silently screaming, "DON'T GO." But she went, with joint sincere promises to "stay in touch," and at first, they did. Soon the WhatsApp messages became infrequent until, without either of them really noticing, they finally stopped altogether.

Like so many things in Nicholas's life, the car accident was random. Nicholas had been driving along a Spanish coast road on his way to a winter training camp when it happened. He could still remember very little. Initially, the doctors had told him that it was just a broken arm, however, it never healed properly. He recalled how hard he had tried to get back into training nevertheless he couldn't get to anywhere near to his previous standards and eventually accepted that retirement was inevitable.

Working for Eurosport had been a challenge, but one he had mainly enjoyed. His experience and forensic knowledge of the sport propelled him to be a much sought-after commentator and pundit. He winced as he thought about his periodic clumsiness in some of his commentaries, and he remained baffled as these 'slips' helped to propel him to almost legendary status and, apparently, added to his 'charm'.

The gameshow programme producer had introduced him to his co-presenter. He remembered her as cool, professional and surprisingly tolerant of his frequent/occasional lapses. Over time she started to build up a confidence that he didn't even realise was in him. It became inevitable that they would grow close both professionally, and eventually, personally. The audience had screamed with joy when as a couple they announced, on air, that they were engaged to be married. The programme was a resounding ratings success and Nicholas (although it had been a complete mystery to him why) had built up an almost cult-like following which brought him many offers of jobs, from voiceover contracts to a presenter of documentaries.

Nicholas sighed as he remembered how pleased he was when his new wife agreed to settle in the area where he grew up.
As the clouds gathered and the temperature lowered, Nicholas tried to forcibly push his past thoughts away and focus on the present.
Was Nicholas Davison weird? Perhaps he'll never find out.

Nicholas abruptly became aware that he wasn't alone. He looked up and a broad grin formed.

It was Robin.

Nicholas liked Robin.

-0-

Two years on

"Who was that on the phone, Nicholas love, you were on it for ages? I've got the baby off, he's in his crib in the living room, don't wake him up, it took me ages to get him down."

Nicholas slipped into the kitchen and wiped his hands on a tea towel. He could smell dinner being prepared. "It was Jackie, you know, my agent's PA. I've been invited onto that Friday evening talk show, the one hosted by that Welsh fella."

"Wow, you've accepted, I hope? Who else is on with you? Anyone interesting?"

Nicholas leaned against the kitchen table and stared down at the floor.

"Well, there's a boxer, who I've met a couple of times at dinners and such like... and," Nicholas hesitated, his voice lowered, "a Hollywood actress."

"Ooo, now that's interesting, what's her name?"

"Tracey Albourne-Jones," replied Nicholas still staring hard at the floor.

"Tracey Albourne-Jones? I remember some of the ladies in my breakfast club mentioning her. Didn't she live around here before she got all famous? She would have gone to the same school as you, Preston Park Comprehensive? The ladies said she was just plain Tracey Albourne in those days. She's obviously done well for herself."

"Yes, she has," whispered Nicholas. "I do remember her. We were in the same year."

THE END

Printed in Great Britain
by Amazon

41432247R00086